The Realms of Death

Marie Rowan

Published in 2017 by
Moira Brown
Broughty Ferry
Dundee. DD5 2HZ
www.publishkindlebooks4u.co.uk

ISBN 978-1-5497-4530-0

Dedication:

To Marion McDonald, the kindest and most loyal of friends.

Acknowledgement:

I would like to thank my publisher, Moira Brown, for her professionalism, friendly support, astute comments and wonderfully creative ideas for the cover of this book.

Chapter 1

Duncan Mitchell stood erect, his butler's livery an inch perfect fit, as his eyes roamed ceaselessly over the scene before him. Impressions of colour flashed past him presenting a pointillist blur of an artist's palette in time to the music of the Julian du Limousin Ensemble. All was well. Dinner had been a huge success as always, Mrs Brady and Monsieur Hugo, forming an unlikely tandem in the kitchen. They had been cooking and creating harmoniously in Crosteegan Castle's vast kitchen for the cream of society, surpassing all expectations yet again. The ball was in full swing now under the discreet influence of Julian's choice of music and the quiet ejection of potential drunks under the firm guidance of Mitchell's soft tones and very firm hand on elbow. The two or three usual culprits welcomed the relief of a quiet library, deep leather sofas and excellent brandy near at hand. The ballroom's occupants swayed and moved rhythmically, each movement brilliantly reflected in the mirrored walls.

Mitchell's eyes were suddenly drawn to the many sets of open French windows leading onto the colonnaded terrace. It was late winter but even the chill air was welcome in the rising heat of two hundred bodies dancing as they prepared to welcome in the Old New Year. The Twelfth of January was held sacrosanct at Crosteegan.

Mitchell suddenly moved with deceptive speed as he soundlessly summoned the under-butler to take his place and then took off like lightening through the green baize door at the end of the Great Hall and down the back stairs into the kitchen.

"Maddy?" he called and Mrs Brady's floury hand pointed Mitchell in the direction of Crosteegan's skivvy. Mitchell tore through scullery, then through an ancient oak door and into the long, chilled corridor that led to the wine cellar. He slammed the door shut behind him and cut off the hysterical wailing of the young man now slumped on the stone, cold floor.

"Whitehead, get up!" When the man continued to wail and to remain prostrate on the floor, Mitchell grabbed the six foot three footman under the arms as if he were a feather and yanked him onto his feet.

"He's soiled himself, Mr Mitchell," whispered Maddy. "I brought him in here as soon as he stumbled into the kitchen. Crazy, he was, sir, and talking complete rubbish. Made no sense at all."

"Get someone to fetch him down clean underwear and trousers then make yourself scarce. He's needed upstairs. Where the hell has he been anyway? This time tomorrow, he'll be unemployed. Move, Maddy!" Maddy moved. "And don't come back in here. You've work to do, so do it."

Mitchell dragged the gibbering footman back along the corridor as far as the closed door to the scullery. He turned the oil lamp up. The stench was unbearable. Under no circumstances could it be allowed to filter through to the kitchen. Fortunately, the old door was a tight fit. The footman's shrill voice was being lowered as Roly Whitehead calmed down and realised he was being given the evil eye by Crosteegan's butler.

"Sit on that stool. It's too late now to be worrying about spreading the shit. I'll have someone hand in a bucket of hot water, some soap and an old cloth and a towel. Do what needs to be done and get clean clothes on. Then I'll have the whole story of what you've been up to when I get back here in twenty minutes. After you've washed, dump the soiled clothing in the bucket and let the water do the preliminary soak. Shove it outside as far as possible from the kitchen door." The butler strode through the kitchen a few minutes later on his way back upstairs, his face like thunder, and even the temperamental and extremely voluble French chef looked the other way and for once kept his mouth tight shut.

Once back in the Great Hall, Mitchell seamlessly assumed the persona of the quiet servant who saw to it that Lord and Lady Askaig's abode ran smoothly and with absolute efficiency. Newton had expertly now guided the revellers comprising many Peers of the Realm, Members of Parliament, Captains of Industry, captains whose industrial boats had sunk and thus had achieved sympathetic, favoured status in Her Ladyship's eyes and local bigwigs along to the Long Gallery where a magnificent buffet awaited them with suitable and endless alcoholic beverages to help with its digestion. He waited patiently for Archie Newton, his under-butler, to give him the nod that Whitehead was no longer in a stomach-churning state. Mitchell wanted to interview the footman very badly. He wanted to know why he had seen him racing across the terrace when he should have been serving drinks on the fringes of the ballroom and he especially wanted to know why a young man, completely devoid of imagination, had been totally reduced to a gibbering idiot. Maddy would know something. He would have bet anything that Whitehead had been making for Crosteegan's skivvy and solace. That Mitchell was also Maddy's employer as head and owner of The Mitchell Detective Agency gave him an additional lever when it came to finding out what Roly Whitehead had said. She had got hold of him and steered him away from the kitchen into the passageway while his nerves had been shattered and before common sense had begun to kick in. Any unguarded comments would now be filed away in her very analytical mind. Even Roly would by now be regretting giving way to panic. There were more servants in Crosteegan Castle than you could shake a stick at and Mitchell knew they were well-drilled enough to cope if he himself disappeared for ten minutes. He looked on with satisfaction as the guests now rested and ate, the gaslight shimmering off the crystal dishes, bowls and epergne adorning the damask-covered tables stretching the length of the gallery. The ensemble played softly in the background as the servants catered discreetly to the guests every need. The Askaigs were frequent and tastefully lavish entertainers. Mitchell caught Archie Newton's eyes and quietly joined him at the wide, glass doors of the Gallery entrance.

"I take it Whitehead now has everything he needs?" Mitchell glanced sideways at Newton as he spoke. The under-butler nodded.

"It's all been sent down, sir." Mitchell moved back a little till he could see down the length of the Gallery but he and Newton were more or less out of sight. Archie Newton had followed him.

"Do you know anything at all about this, Archie? A normally placid, reliable footman who should have been outside only briefly to deliver toddy to the coachmen is suddenly bolting along the terrace and screaming like a banshee."

"Westway says he knocked him over as he was collecting empty glasses on the terrace. Didn't even stop running for a moment."

"God Almighty! Not the rummers!" Newton nodded.

"How many?"

"Five, barrel-shaped bowls and matching decanter. Smashed to smithereens."

"Not the Georgian ones and the three palin-necked rings decanter?"

"I'm afraid so, sir."

"Were there any guests involved?" asked Mitchell. Things were getting progressively worse.

"None. The terrace was momentarily clear just then."

"Thank God for that," muttered Mitchell. "That was probably why I had a clear view of him." But Newton had more to say.

"One of the stable-boys was running behind him trying to catch him but the lad had the good sense to stop when they came to the terrace. It seems Roly had taken the dog-cart earlier on without permission, of course, and had just returned it in a manner of speaking. He had stopped it at random in the mews and then hared back here as if the devil himself was on his heels."

"And screaming fit to be tied!" said Mitchell.

"Thank God the orchestra was playing a reel very boisterously and it seems he got away with I, sir." Mitchell could feel the anger rising within him again as Newton spoke.

"So, Archie, apart from destroying most of a set of Georgian rummers and its decanter, he also quit his post earlier in the evening and stole the dog-cart. At the same time or shortly after, he lost his sanity and shit himself. Have you any idea what those rare glasses and decanter are worth - were worth?" The two men were silent for a few minutes before Archie dared to broach the subject again.

"It's not like him to be so reckless."

"Feel free to write that in his testimonial for he'll certainly not get one from me nor anyone else who counts in this castle. Come the dawn, he's out." Newton knew that there was really no alternative. But Mitchell's mind was, as always, needing to know all the details. "Have you any idea at all what caused it? Not that it really matters. I'll get it out of him before he's shown the castle gates but I'd like to have at least an idea of what to expect from him and how to question him."

"I've no idea. I couldn't even hazard a guess for he's never done anything like this before." That was as much a plea for mitigation as Newton could muster but he knew it was hopeless.

"He wouldn't be stinking the passage leading to the door of the wine cellar or anywhere else right now if he had." Mitchell's face was impassive but his bearing said Whitehead was in for a very rough time. He doubted if Lord Askaig would feel any different. "What did the head coachman have to say about Whitehead having misappropriated the dog-cart?"

"Dougie Cranston appeared while some of us were brushing up as best we could the shattered pieces of glass. He didn't even know it had gone until the stable-lad gave him the bad news after he'd seen Roly commit virtual suicide on the terrace. Seems he'd had it backed into a dead-end just off the drive to accommodate all the visiting carriages along the main drive. With dozens of carriages expected to remain till the early hours, Dougie needed all the space he could muster." Mitchell knew there was no point in talking about it or speculating as to what had caused it all. The whole episode was completely bizarre and as staff were plentiful, he decided that it would be business as usual while he had a word with Maddy. Whitehead could wait unless he was more rational but Mitchell had a very bad feeling about the whole affair. Both men turned their attention to the small dais situated by the wall on the window side of the Long Gallery and halfway down the room. Lady Askaig was already standing there, her husband seated casually at her feet, legs clamped firmly on the floor for support. There was no sense in having parties, that titled couple believed, if you did not enjoy them yourself. A rabid believer in the old pagan ways, it was his duty to his forebears, Lord Askaig maintained, to keep their old religion alive. The Rev John McDougall sat shoulder to shoulder beside him as always, demonstrating his religious pragmatism, both men's beliefs bolstered by copious amounts of their native drink. Lady Askaig's toast never varied. It was short, sweet and much appreciated for that. It marked the end of the frolics and the start of an hour-long's gradual winding down as Mrs Brady and Monsieur Hugo's buffet talents were deeply appreciated and savoured. Nothing was ever rushed at Crosteegan and nobody, but nobody, ever rose on Old New Year's Day before noon except His Lordship himself. Mitchell cast his eyes round to choose which of the inebriated guests he could reasonably hint at as being the Georgian glass disaster culprits. Nothing really changed. No-one would even think of leaving for at least an hour and that would give Mitchell time to sort out the whole episode below stairs. Crosteegan Castle's domestic arrangements flowed like a silken stream due to Mitchell's management of personnel and he was now taking it as a personal insult what Roly Whitehead had done. The Askaigs paid well for the best service which was extremely unusual in itself and Mitchell was there to ensure it was delivered. Roly Whitehead had never failed him before and that was what worried Mitchell.

"I'm off, Archie. I'll be as quick as I can. Once I've sorted out this business with Whitehead, I'll go to the library where I've put a few guests who've drunk too much to sleep it off. If they're able to walk unaided, I'll bring

8

them along here and they can enjoy the meal. Otherwise we'll get something light taken to them." Newton nodded and moved silently a few steps into the Long Gallery. He looked at the well-fed revellers in front of him and suppressed a grin at the mental picture of Lord Askaig's curling team attempting to defeat the one from Eddleston that afternoon.

Mitchell strode through the kitchen, now more in clearing-up mode than when he had last ripped through it. Mrs Brady was seated in her little alcove drinking her favourite lemon tea while the French chef, hired always for special, grand occasions when numbers were somewhat daunting, scribbled his evening's culinary observations in a small leather-bound notebook, a large part-eaten slice of fried dumpling - Mrs Brady's own secret recipe - by his other hand. Bodies moved at an alarming speed to and fro, each servant concentrating solely on his or her allotted task. Mitchell nodded to Maddy and she slipped quietly outside and into the chill night air. Mitchell firmly closed the kitchen door behind them.

"If Whitehead's anything other than dead," he said tersely, "he's in deep trouble." Maddy sighed her agreement and pulled the shawl she had slipped off the hook behind the scullery door tighter round her head and shoulders. For a moment she longed for her place as skivvy in the scullery as the bitter cold bit deep.

"He's still breathing, Mr Mitchell, but rather rapidly. Not seriously rapidly, I mean, but he's definitely seriously disturbed."

"By what? The knowledge that he'll be working for nothing for the rest of his life to pay for five shattered Georgian glasses and matching decanter? That bit of information, though, goes no farther, Maddy," warned Mitchell. Maddy understood only too well.

"The Earl of Kingscartner?" she suggested. That Peer of the Realm was one of the usual chosen miscreants. Mitchell and Mrs Brady had a list of such people that they worked through. Vague hints only when asked by their employers who were too well-bred to ask the guilty party for replacements. If the fact that the guilty party had never offered to replace what had been broken ever occurred to the Askaigs, they bore no grudges. They also knew their staff at Crosteegan were too well-trained and careful to do anything other than chip very small pudding basins. But only Mitchell, Cook and Maddy knew about the existence of the list, Maddy as a member of The Mitchell Detective Agency having seen it once purely on a need-to-know basis.

"Quite so. Now, what's Roly Whitehead been saying? Start at the beginning. If he's pegged out by the time you reach the end of your narrative, good," said Mitchell.

"He's in no danger of that, sir, just of going mad. Otherwise, I expect he's quite healthy. If you sit on that wall-seat, Mr Mitchell, I'll get us both some fried dumpling. That should keep us warm while I tell you his story." But Mitchell was shaking his head most emphatically.

"Forget the dumpling and the seat." They both looked at the glistening film of ice covering it and opted to lean against the door. "Start from where he collapsed into your arms, Maddy."

"Well, he didn't actually collapse into my arms, Mr Mitchell." Maddy suddenly remembered Duncan Mitchell, owner of The Mitchell Detective Agency, was very keen on reports being straight to the point and no waffling. "I heard banging on the door, sir. We keep it locked at night in case." She stopped suddenly. "Right. You know about that. Yes, well, I opened it, saw Roly Whitehead gasping for breath between screams of horror and I dragged him along the floor for he'd collapsed by this time, and although he's over six feet tall he's built like a whippet, so it was easy enough. Brushed his face on the flagstones once or twice but scratches heal in no time and he can always blame it on that under-gardener's black cat. It's got a new litter and Roly's very fond of animals." Mitchell glowered, Maddy got straight to the point. "At first I couldn't make out a word he said and I was also put off by the stench coming from him. I'm told you can smell fear if you're very sensitive."

"I know what you smelled, Maddy, so just get on with what you asked him and what his replies were, coherent or otherwise. I assume he's still in the passageway?"

"That he is. Mrs Brady gave him some dumpling when he was all cleaned up as a sort of comforter- substitute. She didn't think you would allow alcohol as you might want him to work upstairs until he was dismissed from the castle." Maddy sniffed but her accusing look quickly faltered under Mitchell's extremely hostile gaze. He remained silent and Maddy wondered briefly why she felt

11

guilty when she was not in fact responsible for anything wrong at all. "I thought if he talked about it, it might help."

"While you were dragging him along the freezing cold passageway?"

"Yes." Mitchell nodded his approval. He had always much admired those Georgian rummers and the decanter. Whitehead was a philistine and he felt no sympathy for the predicament the footman was in. It was the worst occasion of the calendar for a servant to lose his head and Mitchell would take most of the blame going. Wee swine, he thought sourly.

"So what have we learned, Maddy?"

"I'll give you a brief summary, shall I? Write it down later for you, Mr Mitchell?"

"No need, Maddy, for this is not an official case for the agency. In other words, nobody's paying us. But as Crosteegan's butler, I would appreciate a brief report with all the salient facts included."

"Roly told me he had taken a tray of drinks round to the mews where the carriage drivers had all gathered as usual. On the way back, he saw the dog-cart backed into a bay just off the drive. On impulse he thought he'd have a go at driving it. Just along a bit of the drive and back. But the horse - Young Toby - had other ideas and before Roly knew it, the dog-cart was haring off down the drive and onto the Peebles Road. You remember Young Toby had been raised just outside Innerleithen, sir, and that road runs straight there after Peebles."

"First-footing, was it?" asked Mitchell coldly. Maddy suppressed a giggle with difficulty.

"Anyway, Roly managed to stop the horse, maybe Young Toby's a pony, I don't know, but anyway he managed to stop it and turn it round just beyond the Brangle House estate lodge."

"And then what?"

"Roly ran into the woods and threw up. Not the sort of calling card you should leave by the side of the public highway," said Maddy nippily. "That's when Roly felt himself being grabbed from behind. He glanced back and saw a dreadful, ugly, bloodied creature. Black from head to toe, claws raking the air as it tried to rip the flesh from his bones. Roly managed somehow to reach the dog-cart and the rest is history."

"And you have been his mentor all his days so it was Maddy Pearson he made for." Maddy nodded in agreement.

"He's a cousin, sir. Roly's a few years older than me but males mature later than females in mind and body."

"I must try and remember that hot tip," said Mitchell sarcastically. "And do you believe him, Maddy?"

"No, sir, and I assume you don't either."

"Quite so. Am I right in thinking he is now fully kitted out?"

"Not really, Mr Mitchell, almost but not quite. Roly isn't wearing his coat. I've got it in the scullery hanging over a small set of ladders. We keep that little stool in the passageway to help me reach the high shelves and the ladders for reaching the window. It gets very steamed-up in there on a busy evening like this. It'll also get rid of the smell."

"For god's sake, is his coat covered in shit too?" But Mitchell did not wait for an answer. He quickly opened the kitchen door and bawled,

"Someone get upstairs fast and fetch Whitehead's second-best coat!"

"Oh no, sir," said Maddy quickly, "it's not covered in that. It's only the back of his coat that's the problem, Mr Mitchell. You hauled him up and he was facing you so you didn't see it. The back is covered in blood, sir, - and it's not Roly Whitehead's blood!"

Chapter 2

Duncan Mitchell badly needed some sleep. He knew that. He also knew he had no chance of getting it. All night he had puzzled over one major question that needed answering. Where had the bloodied apparition gone? But now he had two. Where had the blood-drenched coat gone? He had no answer to either question and he had exhausted every possible or probable avenue. Maybe it had indeed been taken with the rest of the laundry, as simple as that. The laundry woman lived out so it would be some time before he found out. He stood up, shrugged on his heavy travelling cloak and carefully locked the door of his sitting-room behind him. Crosteegan was a vast and lovely house both inside and out. He paused by one of the tall windows and admired the snow-etched Celtic knots in the garden below, bare of flowers and herbs yet the design clearly picked out by the snow-fall of the past few days. The acres of parkland as far as the eye could see were blanketed with snow but the paths within the walled garden were kept brushed clear as Lady Askaig was an inveterate stroller there regardless of the weather. Mitchell's attention was caught by two dark figures as they walked purposefully across the deep snow heading for Home Farm. Lord Askaig and his land steward. His Lordship lived by his conviction that a brisk walk was all it took to cure a hangover. Mitchell expected them to break into a run any minute for that was also one of His Lordship's cures. Roly Whitehead had been extremely lucky. 'A boyish prank brought on by his well-documented sympathy for animals especially Young Toby.' His Lordship had decreed. Mitchell had conveyed the aristocratic decision to the footman. Somehow, the butler had neglected to mention the Georgian glasses and decanter. Having trained as an advocate in his younger days, Lord Askaig, on been told of the bloodied apparition in the woods, had declared that he had had his fill of the law and Roly Whitehead's experiences with the supernatural were best dealt with by Mrs Brady and a bottle of some nasty-tasting liquid or failing that, Mitchell was to inform the police. Under no circumstances was Mitchell to allow Whitehead to be arrested as it was His Lordship's turn to provide both refreshments and footmen at the curling match in the afternoon. Roly might be competent and no more at serving but he was an expert reader of the game of curling and Crosteegan's only hope of winning against the village short of outright cheating.

Mitchell walked sedately down the pantry stairs as befitted the most important servant in the castle and this mode also accommodated to perfection his own lingering hangover. My God, he thought, but that old dowager's lady's maid could fairly put it away. The annual lock-in in the butler's pantry after the ball had begun ten years previously as a select affair. The participants were still select but their choice of drink was definitely not. Mitchell had woken that morning from the odd half-hour's sleep he had managed to snatch to find himself in the midst of a mountain of empty bottles and several flagons of cider.

"Ready?" That was not so much a question as an order to the two people standing by the outside door of the kitchen. Maddy and Roly straightened to attention. "Now we'll seek out the constable at Eddleston and tell him what took place last night. What he decides to do is what we'll abide by." The clock chimed 8.30am and the head kitchen-maid had everything under control for breakfast. Mrs Brady never cooked breakfast. The family and guests, and that morning there were plenty of them, all generally breakfasted between 9am and 10.30am. Not on that special day, never. Breakfast, though, still had to be cooked on the off-chance someone appeared looking for it. But Lord Askaig never varied his routine and always ate his in the breakfast room alone and at 7.45am prompt. "Roly, there is no need for you to speak of anything other than what you saw in the woods. You took Young Toby for a bit of exercise to calm him down. Your inexcusable lapse has no bearing on anything beyond Crosteegan's gates. There is no need to voice it abroad that the staff of this castle lack discipline." Maddy glowered at Roly. "Maddy, you are more than capable of using your own judgement as to what needs to be said to the constable."

The three servants walked out of the kitchen garden and on through a door in the high wall surrounding it. Their route took them north of the main drive and joined the Peebles to Edinburgh road some three hundred yards beyond the lodge. It was the Peebles Road or the

Edinburgh Road depending which side of the road you were on. Crosteegan was situated on the Edinburgh to Peebles side. It was Wednesday, an ordinary working day, and after crossing the road, they kept close into the verdant verge as the horse-drawn traffic flowed back and forth. It was a dangerous and busy road at the best of times but that day the rutted ice made both driving and walking extremely hazardous. It was with some relief that after a mile or so they eventually left it behind as the small stone hump-backed bridge on their left led them on into the short main street of Eddleston village itself. Its tiny cottages lining the narrow street were half-hidden under the covering of snow and only the drifting smoke from the chimneys told that life did actually exist there. It was indeed a very beautiful village, thought Maddy proudly.

Mitchell stood and looked along the one hundred yards or so that separated the bridge and the far end of the street, its cottages grouped tightly together for comfort, it seemed, with the railway station the last building on the left. Mitchell strode up to the police station and knocked loudly. They were expected as a page-boy had been dispatched by Lord Askaig's secretary an hour earlier with a brief summary of Roly's experience in the woods just south of Brangle House lodge the previous evening. Constable Paterson invited them into the small room that served as an office and tea was quickly produced by his wife. Regardless of why they were there, the three newcomers belonged to Crosteegan Castle. Maddy handed over a seed cake from Mrs Brady and business finally commenced.

"The Old New Year," said the constable, "brings out the craziness in people. So what's this all about? What brought a footman from Lord Askaig's household out onto the Edinburgh and Peebles Road driving a dog-cart when his job's indoors?" Three pairs of eyes regarded Roly closely. Roly swallowed hard.

"It was like this, Constable Paterson." He took a very deep breath and tried to remember to stick to the few facts that did not tell of anything to do with Lord Askaig's household. "I was told to take some refreshment - hot toddy - out to the coachmen. There were a great many of them last night so I had to make several journeys. I always do it."

"But last night was slightly different I'm led to believe by Mr Rough, His Lordship's secretary." The policeman pointed to the letter on the table from the castle. "How was it different, Roly? And why?"

"Young Toby." Roly looked at the other three as if that should explain it all.

"That smart wee horse from Innerleithen way?" Roly nodded at the policeman.

"That's him. Each time I passed I noticed he was acting up a bit. He was still between the shafts of the dog-cart. I thought he just needed a wee bit of a run out to settle him so I jumped in and drove him down the driveway. Young Toby, though, had got the bit between his teeth in every way, and at the end of the drive, he turned into the road and headed down towards Peebles." The policeman nodded.

"Makes sense him being a young horse and coming from down that way. Through Peebles and then onto Innerleithen."

"That's what I thought. I managed to stop him just beyond the lodge at Brangle and then eventually brought him back to the castle." Mitchell and Maddy were both trying to gauge Constable Paterson's thoughts. The policeman thought for a minute before looking once more at Roly.

"Fine. Now the missing bit that explains why you're here."

"I'd got a bit of a fright, knew I shouldn't be in the dog-cart or even out of the grounds and I felt sick. I ran quickly into the woods. Suddenly I felt something grab me from behind." Roly was quickly losing his healthy complexion.

"Something or somebody?"

"Something, definitely something. It was really dark in there, almost black."

"But the harsh, bright light from the snow on the ground is blinding, lights up the whole place," commented the policeman.

"I know," agreed Roly, "but not underneath the trees. The snow doesn't reach there because of the overhanging branches. It was pitch black. That horrible thing just rose up out of the darkness and was trying to get me." Roly was becoming slightly hysterical once more and his distress was upsetting Maddy. But one glare from Mitchell warned her to leave things to the policeman.

"Describe what you saw, Roly," he said to the footman.

"Just claws, grab, grabbing at me."

"And these claws, were they attached to something?" asked Constable Paterson.

"Of course they were!" shouted Roly. He knew when he was not being believed. Another deep breath and Roly lowered his voice once more. "A monster, they were attached to a shapeless monster. It was entirely black, a raging monster."

"And did this monster say anything?"

"It was behind me, Constable Paterson. I just had a quick look back at it but it was making kind of growling, moaning noises as I ran."

"And then what?"

"I ran even faster."

"Did it follow you?"

"I don't think so. Anyway I didn't hear any branches breaking behind me and I didn't stop to listen. I jumped into the dog-cart and Young Toby took off at the double."

"And where did you say all this happened?"

"About a hundred yards or so beyond the lodge on the Peebles side." The policeman looked at Mitchell and Maddy before speaking again.

"Well, it seems to me, Roly, you've been the victim of a poacher having a bit of a laugh at your expense." Roly thought better than argue as Mitchell's face was telling him that he thought the whole episode a complete waste of his precious time. He also knew Mitchell had a meeting in Peebles later on to discuss some friendly games of football and, as the manager of the FSV, that could rake him in a bit of much needed cash for the team and the last thing he needed was to be tied up in Eddleston on what he regarded as a wild goose chase.

"Maybe, Mr Patterson, but what about the blood on my coat? Do you think it came from some dead rabbits or something?"

"As I'm told your coat has vanished, son, we'll never know. In the wash, maybe, Maddy?" Maddy agreed this was a reasonable assumption as the maids at Crosteegan washed constantly anything they saw. "I'm sorry to say, Roly, that if you appear in any inn within five miles of here, you'll be the butt of every monster joke going. Have either of you, Mr Mitchell or Maddy, anything to say that might shed some light on this? We'll do a spot of searching the area. The note from Lord Askaig's secretary said we could use a dozen or so of the estate hands."

"His Lordship is anxious that this should be cleared up as soon as possible, Constable Paterson. I think Roly put it very well. We're very grateful for your interest in this and we'll go now and let you get on with investigating this incident. I'll have the men sent down right away. Roly can wait by the Crosteegan Lodge and then he can direct all of you to as near the spot as he can remember, bearing in mind, as he said, it was very dark within the woods. If you all start directly then Roly will be able to join Crosteegan's curling team's outing to Portmore Loch." Hands were shaken all round as Mitchell, Maddy and Roly reached the door.

"Great ice today, I'm told, Mr Mitchell," said the constable who was an annual spectator. Great excuse for all Lord

Askaig's hungover guests for failing to remain upright, thought that Peer's butler.

Mitchell walked carefully along the road leading back to Crosteegan Castle well aware of Maddy Pearson's silence and Roly Whitehead's lightened mood as they walked together behind him. He would send men down to meet Roly and the constable at the lodge gates, see Maddy on her way through the kitchen garden then settle himself on the cart taking excess bags of potatoes and turnips from the castle garden's storerooms to the greengrocer in Peebles. The icy ground over the last few weeks had meant a lull in his football team's games, a drop in income but a welcome respite in his workload outwith the castle. Being Lord Askaig's butler and manager of the FSV football team plus being owner of The Mitchell Detective Agency meant no time could be wasted. He was heading along the three miles to Peebles to discuss a potential series of matches with the managers of other teams in the district once the thaw had set in. He would also look in at The Wild Duck Inn to meet the team and also to see if any messages had been left there for the Detective Agency. He would come back to Eddleston by the afternoon train. Mitchell stopped by the small gate in the wall that surrounded the vast expanse of the Crosteegan estate.

"Right now, Roly, you carry on and wait at the lodge and I'll send the men down this way to meet you. Won't take them more than a few minutes. The constable's already on his way as I can see behind us so you just do your best to help and then it's back on duty for you. I'm going into Peebles on business so Mr Newton will be in charge.

You'll be going with the curling party after lunch so keep your mind on the job and remember that it's Lord Askaig who gives you board and lodgings plus your wages so his needs come before Young Toby's."

"Yes, Mr Mitchell." With that subdued answer to that minor rebuke, Roly trudged on by himself through the ice and snow. Mitchell closed the wrought-iron gate once both he and Maddy were through and they walked on up to the great house where he could already see the men milling quietly around by the series of outbuildings to the rear waiting for their orders.

"All right, Maddy, out with it." Maddy hesitated just for a moment before speaking.

"Do you think the search will bring something to light, Mr Mitchell?" she asked.

"Probably not. As Roly said, it all took place in amongst the trees. No snow, loads of dust and broken branches. A hopeless task."

"No monster?" she suggested.

"I'm sure the boy thought he saw one but even the Old New Year was never about monsters."

"Halloween's not about them either," said Maddy in agreement.

"So what's worrying you, Maddy, why the puzzled look? Maddy sighed.

"It's Roly's story, sir. We didn't believe it last night and I definitely don't believe it now. Why do you think he's making it all up, Mr Mitchell?"

"Because I know Roly and I know young men. He was going to meet a girl and he's been around dog-carts and horses since he could walk. He knows how to handle them, skittish or placid. It was probably as the constable suggested. The blood-stains were made by a poacher swinging a dead rabbit or two at Roly as he fled," said Mitchell. Maddy mumbled her agreement.

"She works at Brangle House. The girl."

"I thought so. Here, watch that ankle of yours. The ground on this part of the path is very uneven. When are you due back at the Royal Infirmary for the post-operation check-up?" asked Mitchell frowning.

"Tomorrow, sir. But, Mr Mitchell, Roly was definitely frightened to death last night."

"He was, yes. And what else is bothering you Maddy?" Mitchell had great faith in his latest employee of The Mitchell Detective Agency's intuition.

"It was what he was screaming when I first dragged him into the passageway and what he also then said when I came back with you. It had changed very slightly."

"But significantly, Maddy?"

"I think so, sir," she said reluctantly.

"In what way?" Mitchell had stopped and Maddy now stood beside him looking up at the butler's inscrutable face.

"At first he kept screaming that he was clawing at him. Later, when you appeared, it changed to **it** was clawing at him and that's the word - **it** - he has used ever since." Mitchell said nothing for a few moments.

"And that was after he had had a chance to think clearly, to rearrange his thoughts. It might mean everything or nothing. Let's see what the search throws up." He began walking again as he spoke. "The whole thing's probably not worth all the bother. Possibly it was the girl's father dealing with an unwanted suitor in a very novel and spur-of-the-moment way." They both laughed and parted at the door of the kitchen garden.

Mitchell hopped off the cart at the Northgate in Peebles and walked in under the stone archway that separated the front yard of The Wild Duck Inn from the street. A quiet drink, a team meeting in the back parlour which he had already reserved and then back to Eddleston on the afternoon Edinburgh train. No time for the other team business unfortunately as not all of the managers could attend, it seemed. All quite leisurely and most welcome after the hectic few days at Crosteegan and no respite in view there until Saturday when most of the guests were due to leave. There were always at least a dozen extra guests at the castle apart from the visiting extended family plus unmarried ones and their guests.

"Mr Mitchell!" Mitchell smiled and walked over to the landlord. The landlord, John Melford, kept all correspondence for The Mitchell Detective Agency.

"Is everything ready?" Mitchell asked and accepted his usual glass of malt whisky. Mitchell always ordered food and drink in a modest way for the members of his team who had all managed to slip away for an hour from their daily work.

"Of course, Mr Mitchell, but there's someone wanting a word with you. I've put him in the small parlour. The team's already gathering in the big parlour at the back." Mitchell passed his glass with the remaining whisky to the landlord who placed it on a high shelf. "It's the Detective

Agency the man wants." That brought a definite smile to Mitchell's face. Money coming in might just now be a distinct possibility and that would be good news to pass on to the team. It might even pay for transport for a few away games. Mitchell quickly entered the small parlour.

"Ah, Mr Cairns, I'm told you would like a word with me." Mitchell shook hands with one of the local solicitors and sat down opposite the lean, pinched face man he had known for the ten years he had been at Crosteegan Castle.

"I learned from one of my junior clerks that there was to be a short meeting of the football team here and I thought I might be able to intercept you. I know how tied up you must be at the castle." That clerk was Mitchell's least effective player but great at keeping everybody happy.

"So how may I help you, Mr Cairns?"

"I would like a confidential word with you in your capacity as the owner of The Mitchell Detective Agency with a view to enlisting your services." That was music to Mitchell's ears.

"Certainly, Mr Cairns, my agency's expertise is at your service. Please tell me how we can help." Using 'we' always made it sound as if business was booming and that Mitchell employed a goodly but select force of agents to tackle all the many cases that came the agency's way. "Confidential is the agency byword, Mr Cairns."

"A bit of discreet enquiring, Mr Mitchell, that's all." Mitchell managed to keep the interested look on his face and the disappointed one firmly out of sight. "It must be very discreet. That is why, knowing your record as Lord Askaig's most trusted servant, I was able to reassure my client of your understanding of the phrase 'absolute discretion'. Mitchell smiled and accepted the compliment with a slight inclination of his head. No need to explain to Mr Cairns that Mitchell's discretion had never been put to the test in the service of either Lord or Lady Askaig.

"I understand completely, Mr Cairns. Please continue, sir," said Mitchell. Business, however small, was business when you were getting perilously close to being extremely low on funds. The cadaverous-looking solicitor coughed quietly before beginning.

"My client's husband has failed to return from a week's sojourn in the capital - a business one, of course," added the solicitor hastily.

"And naturally your client is a little anxious for his health," said Mitchell quietly with his expected discretion. The solicitor nodded in agreement.

"He was expected some days ago but as the week has now become ten days, my client thinks that perhaps a little nudge from you would bring him back once more into the bosom of his family."

"And why, if I may ask, would one of your clerks or even a member of the family not take the short journey to Edinburgh and remind the lady's husband of his familial duties?" The solicitor and Mitchell both exchanged men-of-the-world glances but, for business reasons, an explanation had to be forthcoming. Mitchell waited.

"My client and yours assuming you accept the case?"

"I will," said Mitchell much to the solicitor's obvious relief.

"Good. Mr James Sheddon of Angleford House avails himself of the delights of the capital on numerous occasions throughout the year and whilst doing so, might as well be in the upper reaches of the Amazonian rainforest as his whereabouts and activities in Edinburgh during these sojourns are completely unknown. Unfortunately this time an unexpected and urgent matter of business has arisen and his signature is required on numerous very important documents as soon as possible. Mr Mitchell, we need you to find him and bring him back."

"Has he ever been overdue before, Mr Cairns?"

"Frequently!" The solicitor regretted his loss of detachment immediately and hurried on. "It's the papers, Mr Mitchell, they have to be signed and that is what has occasioned the need to locate him as soon as possible. I've a list of haunts that might just produce something but..." Mr Cairns produced an envelope which Mitchell assumed contained the list.

"I quite understand," he said. "These are the unofficial ones that Mrs Sheddon suspects but doesn't voice. Leave the list with me, sir, and I'll deal with it. Discretion guaranteed."

"If you send in your bill, Mr Mitchell, it will be paid immediately. That is Mrs Sheddon's way." Mitchell was very glad to hear it and somehow felt rather sorry for Mrs Sheddon whom he had welcomed several times to Crosteegan Castle. Mitchell watched as the solicitor hurried along the short, dark corridor and out through the back door.

Mitchell's smile was broad as he stepped back into the lounge-bar and accepted the glass of whisky kept on the shelf for him. It was now a little noisier and he looked around him before heading for the meeting in the big parlour.

"They're celebrating, Mr Mitchell, a new baby for Dodie Spiers and his wife." Mitchell shook hands with the Brangle House estate lodge-keeper.

"Another baby, Dodie. Congratulations. And how's Lizzie?"

"She's fine, Mr Mitchell, and it's babies - two of them. One of each kind - again! The hardest part isn't feeding children, it's the walking up and down waiting for them to appear. With twins, it's always twice as long. They don't just tumble out together, you know. And it always seems to be the dead of winter."

"So it's a big fire and a dram or two while you wait?" Mitchell saw no hardship in that. Dodie shook his head.

"I get outside as soon as it starts for I can't stand the racket. Walk up and down, I do, and stay well clear till it's all over. But last night was no night for that, I can tell you. I thought I'd never thaw out."

"So there's now a well-worn rut in the drive up to Brangle House," laughed Mitchell slipping a guinea into Spiers' waistcoat pocket for the new-born twins.

"Many thanks, Mr Mitchell," said Spiers. "Because of the ice on the drive, I kept to the grassy verge by the main road. Along the road in front of the lodge, back and forth all that long night I walked and not a soul coming or going there to talk to and take my mind off it all after Lord

Askaig's guests had all passed earlier in the evening."

Bells started ringing in Mitchell's head.

"And when, Dodie, did the babies finally put in an appearance?" he asked.

"Just as the estate clock chimed midnight." So Roly had never been near the lodge. Now why, wondered Mitchell, had Roly found it necessary to lie?

Chapter 3

The tea was hot and strong. Mitchell savoured every drop of it as he sat at the long table in the near stillness of the Servants Hall. He eyed the cold beef sandwiches piled on a plate before him by Mrs Brady for no more than a few seconds before tucking in. He thought momentarily of the delicious spread he had ordered for the team in The Wild Duck but had not stayed to enjoy. It had already been paid for and Mitchell now hoped the case of the naughty husband would prove to be a nice little earner and good publicity for the agency among folk who could afford to pay at least part of his fee before he began work on the case.

"More tea, Duncan?" Mitchell nodded and Jenny Brady poured for both of them. "Is Maddy getting ready?" asked the cook as she took her seat opposite him.

"It's very kind of you, Jenny, to send that food parcel along to Dodie's wife." It was 'Duncan' and 'Jenny' only when other servants were absent.

"New babies or no, the family will still expect her to be on her feet cooking for them. That should take care of that for a good few days."

"I think Maddy was just hoping for a few jars of honey and jam and maybe a small cake to welcome the new arrivals," said Mitchell.

"And that's what I've put in the basket. She's going to see her friend in Eddleston as it's that girl's aunt who's just given birth so she can kill two birds with the one stone. She can get a few of the boys in the family to come here and collect soup and some big pots of stew. That'll keep them going for a bit. A few dozen eggs and some butter and a couple of loaves of bread will mean very little cooking is necessary. Here she comes. Right, Maddy, just take the basket and off you go. Now no lingering for we've a dinner to make," said the cook sternly although as skivvy, Maddy was never allowed to stray anywhere near the huge ovens.

"The vegetables and potatoes are all ready, Mrs Brady. I'll be back as soon as I can." Maddy pulled her large shawl over her coat and hurried out of the door.

That had been quite a shock and no mistake, thought Mitchell, thinking back over his conversation with Dodie Speirs. So Roly had been lying all the time? But exactly how much of his story had been false? All of it? Some of it? Mitchell was now sending Maddy out alone to find out and tomorrow she was to work for the agency on the missing husband one in Edinburgh. He thought of her carrying that heavy basket down the icy drive and hoped she would be careful for the ground underfoot was treacherous and her ankle had not completely healed after her operation. But Maddy had told him she was sure her friend Greta was Roly's girl or at least Roly had high hopes there. Now it was Maddy's job to find out if she knew where he had been during that missing time. Maddy knew she could probably worm it out of Greta Lyall for she never stopped talking and seldom wondered if she should be talking at all.

Once more that day Maddy crossed the little bridge leading into Eddleston village street. The Lyalls lived two cottages beyond Constable Paterson's police station and the quiet street told her that the children of the village were all still in school and the really young ones indoors playing by the fireside. Maddy knew Greta might be at Brangle House but Alice, her sister, was still at home recovering from a severe chest infection and the sisters told each other all their secrets. She rapped loudly and heard footsteps steadily making their way to the door. Everyone at Crosteegan moved quickly and purposefully but not in the village. Greta's mother smiled and stood back for Maddy to go in out of the cold.

"Raw, that's what it is, Maddy, raw. Sit down by the fire and have some hot scones and some milk. What on earth has brought you away from Mrs Brady's warm kitchen and down into the village on a cold, grey day like this?" Maddy helped herself to the buttered scones and milk after resting her heavy basket by the table in front of the fire. She was glad to take the weight off her ankle.

"That, Mrs Lyall, just a few presents for Mrs Speirs from Mrs Brady if you'd be so good as to see that she gets them. And one of the pots of honey and one of jam are for you as well as an Albert cake. Mrs Brady asks if you would send some of the boys up to the castle as soon as you can to collect soup and stew and some other things for that family." Mrs Lyall got the message for everyone in the village knew all the inhabitants of Crosteegan would be at the curling match and no eyes would see what it was in everybody's best interests they did not witness. Mrs Lyall disappeared out of the front door and Maddy and Alice were left alone.

"It's lovely to see you, Maddy. Are you remembering that I'd like to work at the castle? I'm just about fit again. One more week and I'll be fine. I've already started short walks again, long ones next week." Maddy nodded.

"We've had quite a few accidents with torn linen these past few weeks as when there's so much celebrating, folk get careless. I could suggest to our housekeeper through Mrs Brady, if you like that is, that you would be willing to come up to Crosteegan for a few hours a day and do some mending till everything is once again as it was." All the girls in Eddleston were fine needlewomen. "It would at least let her know that you exist and how good and reliable you are." Alice was overjoyed.

"Greta's too taken up with Roly Whitehead to listen when I ask her to put in a word for me at Brangle."

"Roly? Don't tell me they're walking out together?" said Maddy in mock surprise. Alice shrugged.

"Sort of. Well, maybe not anymore after last night for there was a chance they might meet up but it didn't happen. Greta's fault," said Alice.

"Last night? But Roly was on duty. Crosteegan is full to bursting at the moment. He wouldn't be allowed a moment off and he wouldn't dare ask Mr Mitchell."

"Who would?" said Alice and shivered. Maddy felt more than a little annoyed at her hero of the criminal detective business being maligned.

"He's alright once you get to know him. He's very fair, Alice." Alice shrugged again.

"I expect he is but Roly said to Greta he's fearsome." Maddy was still bristling with indignation.

"Yet he was still going to ask Mr Mitchell for time off on the busiest evening of the year just to see his girl?"

"Well, not exactly," said Alice peeping into the covered basket. "He thought he might sneak off down to the lodge at the gates of Crosteegan and say hello to Greta and her friends as they passed by. Maybe he could even get the dog-cart for the short ride, he said, as he couldn't be away for long. Said maybe if he didn't see her there, he would wait opposite the path entrance just for a few minutes," Maddy became the supreme detective at once.

"Path entrance, Alice?"

"They were going to go to Portmore Loch to ice-skate." Maddy was quick to see the implications. Portmore Loch was in the opposite direction from Brangle House lodge. Roly Whitehead had deliberately sent them on a wild goose chase. "It was to be when the girls were relieved of their duties and supposed to be in bed at Brangle House. A few of the kitchen-maids thought it would be fun. But they all just went to bed. It was just a lot of silly talk. Greta sent a note this morning asking how I am and would I get them to explain to Roly if I managed to see folk from the castle." Maddy was thinking out all the implications rapidly. "Will you explain it all to him, Maddy?"

"Oh, yes, Alice, you can count on the fact that I shall certainly be talking to him about it. Now I'd better be getting back. I'll also speak to Mrs Brady and ask her to have a word with our housekeeper about the sewing."

Mrs Brady dozed in the armchair by the fireplace in the Servants Hall. Duncan Mitchell scowled at the scene outside the window as he stood fiercely to attention. Maddy sat at the table where she told of what she had learned in Eddleston. Mitchell hated liars with a vengeance. It told of people wanting control, taking advantage of others and he hated that. He suddenly turned back to the table and sat down opposite Maddy.

"So he really did lie? He had already decided that if he'd missed her or even been too early, he would drive the dog-cart up to the Portmore Loch entrance and listen to hear if voices told him she was there. A very still night and voices carry in the air. Am I right?" She nodded in answer to his question. "But he did much more than just lie, Maddy, he misled the police. Wasted their time." Maddy then cut in.

"But I don't think he expected the law to be involved, in all fairness to him, Mr Mitchell." Maddy suddenly wished she had kept her mouth closed. But Mitchell simply ignored her interruption.

"And by doing that, a man could be lying dead. That so-called moaning monster which Whitehead left in the woods could possibly - probably - have been a cry for help. If Whitehead couldn't face it, he could at least have sent those of us who could off in the right direction to weigh up the situation for ourselves. He lied time and time again to keep us from knowing he had set off to meet his girl. He lied about Young Toby bolting, he lied about the direction he took. He, as far as he knows, didn't meet her possibly because he met the injured man before he had reached the loch. He probably still doesn't know that she was never there. I've sent word of all this to the constable but as it's dark now and the snow is once more falling thickly, the chances are he'll have to wait until morning before another search can be undertaken. He'll maybe attempt a token one but it would be just that. I can guarantee that Roly Whitehead will be out of here and a situation first thing tomorrow. His actions were deliberate even after a considerable time had elapsed and someone might have died because of his selfishness. I'll have a word with Lord Askaig right now and then I've something to discuss with Mrs Brady. You did very well Maddy but right now, make yourself scarce. The others will appear for their evening meal so come back then." Maddy was only too happy to close the scullery door and she hoped for everybody's sake that Constable Paterson and the searchers would not find a body.

Mitchell had asked Mrs Brady to join him in his pantry, door open, voices very low.

"You were saying about our list of possible glass-breakers," said the cook. "Want to update it, I suppose, since the Honourable William Caligula Smythe accidentally shot himself?"

"He probably just beat half a dozen folk to it," said Mitchell wryly. "But yes, Jenny. Any ideas? Local gentry, aristocracy, the sheriff? Someone who's not likely to keep dashing off to the fleshpots of the French Riviera."

"And not anyone connected with the law, Duncan, in case they hear that we sort of hinted that they were involved and try to sue us," said the cook decisively. Jenny Brady tut-tutted.

"Quite so, Jenny, and I'm sure His Lordship won't like us constantly naming the same people. Lady Victoria is sure to notice if we do and her tongue is as sharp as a carving knife and she's even beginning to advise her mother on the guest list," said Mitchell frowning. "Some of His Lordship's merrier cronies are being given the order of the boot."

"Is she now? Marry her off, is the answer to that. And I'll tell you something else, Duncan, a carving knife will have to be well-honed to beat her tongue and she thinks she can bake as well! Instructions only, of course, never a sticky hand in the dough." Both of them shook their heads which meant a sticky time of a different sort for Lady Victoria if she overstepped good breeding and appeared frequently in Mrs Brady's domain.

"Is there anyone new to the district at all?" asked the butler.

"Only Lord Kilmanton who's bought the Low Souldress estate and the Sheddons at Angleford House and the Sheddons aren't new at all. They've owned the house for a great many years but it's been rented out for almost twenty years, long before you came here. The estate and the house really belonged to Mrs Sheddon's father, Sir Michael Lindsay; been in the family for generations and she inherited it from him."

"Have you ever met him, the husband that is?"

"Never met him socially obviously but I've seen him occasionally - in the old days when he was much younger."

"An eye for the ladies, has he?" asked the butler. Mrs Brady looked long and hard at Mitchell.

"Now what is this all about, Duncan?" But Mitchell remained silent. "Alright. Not in the old days, he hadn't, nothing like that. He was from Edinburgh or maybe Glasgow and just appeared now and then when he was romancing the lady."

"Had money?"

"He wouldn't have been allowed through the door if he hadn't but Miss Lindsay had plenty or rather her father had and she was the only child of the marriage."

"Where have they been living since they left here, do you know Jenny?" asked Mitchell. The more he learned from Jenny Brady, the less time it would take to track Sheddon down.

"Glasgow, I'm told. He has ship-building interests there. Money pouring in." Jenny Brady also had a large network of informants whom she never described as gossips. "But we can't add him to our list as he's not very sociable. As you know, she's been here but he hasn't. But then again, Lord Askaig's millions could be a big draw."

"Does he prefer to do his socialising in Edinburgh?" Mitchell suggested.

"So it would seem. I expect, Duncan, that you're trying to track down an errant husband." Mrs Brady laughed at Mitchell's futile attempt at looking innocent. "Well, in the old days while courting Louisa Lindsay, it seems he liked fine dining and a certain other man's wife in Edinburgh.

Now that lady has been widowed recently, I'm told, but I don't know her name. Perhaps old loves die hard and as we know, living in Peebles is nearer Edinburgh than living in Glasgow."

"Thank you, Mrs Brady. It's not the sort of thing The Mitchell Detective Agency would normally undertake but needs must."

"Maybe there's nothing to it at all. High-flying businessmen must find this area very dull especially in the winter," said the cook.

"I expect a few weeks in the year is not much to bear and the lady seems to be quite accustomed to it. I'll go there myself tomorrow and see what's going on - if I manage to track him down."

"I think you're wanted, Duncan, and I'd best be going to see to dinner." Mrs Brady left and Mitchell beckoned Maddy and Roly into his pantry before firmly closing the door.

"I've been dismissed, Mr Mitchell." The stark fact seemed to echo in the butler's spacious quarters for his own bedroom and sitting-room were just off the actual pantry.

"Sit down both of you," he said indicating two chairs situated in front of a well polished mahogany desk. Mitchell took his place on a leather one behind it. Roly was as white as a sheet but he seemed a million miles away from hysteria. Anxiety was consuming him.

"I take it you've been spoken to by Lord Askaig?" Roly nodded.

"Mr Newton took me up. No testimonial. Constable Paterson spoke to His Lordship after the game and I was told Mr Newton would take me to him when everyone had returned to the castle. They said that I had misled the police, made it all up, all except whatever I encountered that left blood all over the back of my coat. Maddy knew about Greta and the loch. Everybody now knows about it. Lord Askaig said as the situation had changed from a spur of the moment prank into deliberately misleading the police, he had no alternative but to dismiss me immediately without a testimonial."

"I presume you're not surprised by that? You've wasted police time and your deviousness might just have cost a man his life. The police might still not believe you about that but they have to spend time investigating it. Now, I have no idea why the two of you are here. Maddy?" Mitchell waited but not for long.

"I've been talking to Roly, Mr Mitchell, and he really needs a testimonial. He knows Lord Askaig had no choice but to dismiss him but Roly won't get another position without a testimonial."

"Not as a footman, he won't," said Mitchell coldly.

"But he's given reliable service for years, Mr Mitchell," Maddy protested.

"And when it suited him, he lied simply for his own benefit. I think the word unreliable is being generous. Your best bet, Mr Whitehead, is to clear out altogether before Constable Paterson sees fit to charge you." But Maddy would not let go as Mitchell knew she wouldn't.

"Mr Mitchell, I've been talking to Roly and I think maybe you should listen to what he has to say." Mitchell shook his head.

"I think I've heard enough of his stories to last me a lifetime. Now, out, both of you. I believe Lord Askaig has no objection to your remaining in the castle overnight, Roly, and that we'll take that as meaning you can have your meals in the Servants Hall as usual." Roly shook his head determinedly.

"No, Mr Mitchell, I'll go right now for I've already packed my bag. I've let everybody down, I know it and I bitterly regret it. Maybe I'll be allowed to say farewell to Young Toby."

"Maybe the word should be 'apologise' and not 'farewell' for you used that animal you profess to be so fond of shamelessly in your web of lies and deceit." Roly was struck dumb as the reality of his situation hit home. But Maddy held his arm.

"Don't go, Roly! Mr Mitchell, sir, ask Roly what really happened last night."

"Another version of this fairy tale? I don't think so," said Mitchell scowling at the skivvy. Maddy ignored him.

"Tell him, Roly. Tell Mr Mitchell for he's a good listener." Maddy's glare dared Mitchell to contradict her before faltering as she realised what she had done.

"All right, speak." Mitchell leaned forward, his elbows on his desk and looked at the young people sitting before him. "Forget the skittish horse nonsense and begin on the way out of Eddleston going north."

"Young Toby was restless, Mr Mitchell, I give you my word on it although you probably think it's worthless now." Mitchell did not contradict him and the silence made Roly hurry on. "I had every intention of skipping off duty for a

43

few minutes or so I admit that. It was just to meet Greta and wave to her at the lodge gates."

"But that's not what happened."

"No, Mr Mitchell. When I reached the lodge gate, Mrs Bently wasn't there so I decided as I was probably a bit late, I'd just take Young Toby a mile or so along the road and maybe catch up with the girls. Young Toby can go like the wind, I knew, so it wouldn't take long and I probably wouldn't be missed. Same with the dog-cart as it was too early for anybody to need a ride home. The road was strangely quiet and although it was icy, I reached the entrance to the loch path in no time at all. I pulled the dog-cart onto the wide verge on the opposite side to avoid the ditch by the path and listened for the sounds of voices up at the loch. I don't know why but I decided to get off." He looked slightly embarrassed and all three knew the reason he was so attracted by the privacy of the woods. "I'd only gone about twelve yards or so into the woods when I realised that I'd better just get back to the castle before I was missed. Panicked a bit, I suppose, and that's when the man tried to grab me from behind. At first I thought I'd snagged my coat on a branch because they were hanging low from the weight of some snow that had filtered through the upper branches." Roly stopped and took a deep breath. Mitchell half expected Maddy to pour him some water from Mitchell's cut glass decanter. "It was a man whose face seemed to be dripping blood all over it, so much so what with that and how dark it was I could hardly make it out as a human form. The head seemed all dashed to bits. I just took off scared out of my wits but all I could hear was branches breaking behind me and this awful moaning. Then it all suddenly stopped just as I reached Young Toby. All except the moaning. Honest to God, Mr Mitchell, Maddy, this is the gospel truth. I stopped, couldn't move, couldn't even jump into the dog-cart. Then I found myself following the moaning back into the woods and that was when I saw them."

"Them? How many?" asked Mitchell quietly.

"Two of them. The injured one and the one helping him or so I thought. Suddenly the other one was battering the man on the ground and then nothing. They were just dark forms and one of them had just melted away into nothing. I went over but the poor man was dead. Unrecognisable. Absolutely lifeless. I waited for a few minutes or so hoping he would start breathing again but nothing, no life was there. I've seen dead bodies before, Mr Mitchell, through illness and accidents, and this person was definitely dead."

"And you had no idea who he was?"

"None. His face was smashed in."

"And why did you come haring back to the castle screaming like a banshee?" asked Mitchell.

"Because he came after me."

"But you just said he was dead." Some of Mitchell's scepticism was returning.

"The other one. He must have been close by me all the time, just out of sight, in amongst the trees. I took off and raced towards the dog-cart with him running alongside me just out of sight behind some bushes. He lunged at me just as I reached the clearing but I turned Young Toby fast and we were racing back along the road within seconds. I glanced back but all was silent, just an empty space. He's after me, Mr Mitchell, for he thinks I saw him and could recognise him again." Roly was shaking with fright once more and Mitchell poured him a very small glass of brandy. Roly smiled his gratitude and Mitchell felt sorry for the boy.

"And could you recognise this man, the attacker?" he asked.

"Absolutely no chance. It was pitch black in amongst those trees. Those people were simply shadows moving about, a dark mass. I thought that if I made it clear I would say nothing about what I had really seen, I would be safe. That's why I tried to make out I had been on the Peebles side of Eddleston."

"So that was why you concocted that elaborate charade of misdirecting the search?" said Mitchell.

"Yes, sir. What has hurt most in all this was the accusation that I had maybe let a man die to save my own skin. He was definitely dead, Mr Mitchell. Nothing I did when I got back here would have saved him. The hysteria was genuine, Maddy, and I'm sorry I've upset everybody. Lord Askaig said he would allow me to stay another day only if the constable required my presence in the second search, instead of just telling him the spot, and if the search went on into the late afternoon."

"Then I expect you should abandon all thoughts of leaving today and see what transpires tomorrow," said Mitchell.

Chapter 4

A slight breeze, bitter and sharp, blew along the railway platform the following morning at Eddleston Station. The ground underfoot had been swept clear of snow and ice and a liberal scattering of salt now did its best to keep potential passengers safe. Mitchell paced up and down in an attempt to keep his feet from freezing within his boots. He had been stationed there for some time in order to see to the comfort and travel arrangements for some of Lord Askaig's departing guests. He now had them comfortably ensconced in the waiting-room where a small fire was making life there more than tolerable. Maddy was in there but not as near the fire. Mitchell would accompany her to Edinburgh. He had high hopes of tracking down the errant husband between them and he was certain his bank balance was guaranteed to swell by the same time the following day.

"Mr Mitchell?"

"Yes Maddy?" said the butler absently without turning to face her. He was looking along the single track back to Peebles and knew the train was due to arrive within minutes.

"Mr Mitchell." Maddy Pearson was persistent and it was her terrier-like quality that would some day put The

Mitchell Detective Agency on the map and a life in service for both of them a thing of the past. "Sir, what are the chances of Constable Paterson and our men finding a body this time?" Mitchell faced his youngest employee.

"Zero, Maddy, zero. Roly said that when he was with the curling party, he managed to slip across the road and had a good look round."

"But he was still only able to search a small area, he said, and hadn't time to do it very carefully," said Maddy aware that her feet already felt like ice.

"That's true, Maddy, but it was the correct area. He was very definite about that. He searched the place where he had last seen the deceased."

"So why didn't he find him then? It was in amongst the trees so there was no chance of that snow last night covering the body."

"Which means that the person who killed him, moved him. And before you ask, I don't know why." That part of the mystery had been bothering Mitchell all through the night.

"Do you think Lord Askaig will change his mind about dismissing Roly, sir? Now that he knows what really happened?" Maddy asked hopefully. But Mitchell shook his head firmly.

"No. His behaviour, quite apart from his involvement in a murder, which murder I might remind you has still to be verified, was completely worthy of instant dismissal."

"But if they find the body?"

"And who's to say that Roly Whitehead, whose coat was covered in blood, did not in fact commit the crime. We have only the somewhat tarnished word of a proven liar that it happened as he said it did."

"Only at the back, Mr Mitchell, his coat was stained only there. To my mind that proves Roly was running away like he said. It must mean something," muttered Maddy. That was another aspect of the whole thing that puzzled Mitchell.

"Here comes the train. You get yourself settled in 3rd Class and I'll join you when I've ushered Lord Askaig's guests into 1st Class."

"Mr Mitchell," said Maddy looking up at her detective hero.

"Yes, Maddy."

"You don't believe Roly did it, do you?"

"No I don't."

"And you do believe his story?"

"Which one? The latest?" Maddy nodded. Mitchell sighed. "Oddly enough I do, now stand back from the edge of the platform as it still has small patches of ice on it." The train came slowly to a halt and Mitchell settled the departing guests with as much care as if they were still in the drawing-room at Crosteegan Castle. Lady Compsten and friend made a point of spreading themselves out and were none too pleased when Mitchell guided the old Dowager Countess of Lochdenny into the seat between them.

"Lord Kilmanton, how good to see you again," she said quite oblivious to the scowls behind her back. Mitchell smiled, looked back as he exited the compartment to find his own seat beside Maddy and had the oddest sensation of déjà vu. Their compartment was empty.

"Something wrong, Mr Mitchell?" asked Maddy, quick to pick up on anything out of the norm.

"No, nothing at all, just a memory awakened but unrecognised."

"You've been all round the world, haven't you, sir? With the army, I mean?" You must have seen many strange sights, places."

"And people, Maddy, and people. Too many, though, for they're all crammed like pages of a book that have become stuck together and are totally meaningless."

"I never thought of it like that, Mr Mitchell," said Maddy wistfully.

"Now we have our own work to do." Maddy coughed slightly before speaking once more.

"Mr Mitchell, instead of paying me for this case with the agency as a detective, I mean, would you speak to Lord Askaig about Roly? I promise that regardless of what his final decision is, I'll accept it." Mitchell tried not to laugh.

"That's a deal, Maddy, though I trust you will still give your instructions concerning this case your best efforts." There was a warning note in the voice of the owner of The Mitchell Detective Agency.

"Absolutely, sir, you can count on that. But I must say I'm very hurt that the thought that I wouldn't even crossed your mind." Mitchell sat in silence, suitably chastened until they reached Waverley Station.

The chill in the air was even worse in Edinburgh as the wind blew in off the North Sea. Siberia! That was probably where it was coming from was Maddy's suggestion as Mitchell bundled her into a hansom on her way to the Royal Infirmary. Time was of the essence and they both had to learn as much as possible before taking the late afternoon train back home. Mitchell also hoped to squeeze in afternoon tea with a certain fascinating Edinburgh schoolteacher of his acquaintance.

Beltane Street was busy with imposing townhouses quietly and expensively overlooking the traffic that swayed back and forth along its wide expanse. Busy but respectfully quiet for the only non-residential occupants of the street were gentlemen's clubs and one ladies club all fitted in snugly near the end of the row. Mitchell hoped that the man he wanted to talk to, the one man who could possibly cut through days of frustrating searching, would be dining there. If not in Edinburgh ostensibly with his regiment, The Black Watch, Major Alan Sinclair could be anywhere in the world for the major was almost free-lance and would crop up before trouble flared and often during it at any hotspot where the army saw fit to send him. But right then, Major Sinclair's knowledge that Mitchell wanted was that pertaining not to a potential war but an errant husband.

Mitchell waited inside the small room that was reserved for members' employees placed discretely just off the main reception area with its wonderful marble floor as the official on the desk sent a page through the pillared, oak-panelled sitting rooms and vast library to inform Major Sinclair that Mr Duncan Mitchell would be pleased if he could spare him a few minutes of his time. The club,

The East of India Planters Club, was a mixture of complete silence and deep-piled carpets. Mitchell had been there before and doubted if a single planter had ever set foot in it or any member had ever been east of India or, in fact, Leith Docks. He faintly heard the soldierly stride of the major crossing the marbled hallway before he entered the room and closed the door quietly behind him. Mitchell rose quickly and they shook hands.

"Sergeant Mitchell, good to see you. It's all arranged and I've had it written down for you." Mitchell smiled and filed the slip of paper into his old leather pocket-book. Another money-spinner but this time a huge one. Mitchell's football team versus the 42nd, The Black Watch.

"Many thanks, Major Sinclair," he said and they both sat down. One good turn had deserved another.

"Now what's this all about, sergeant? You haven't come to see me because of a football match." The army officer's eyes bored into Mitchell with frank curiosity.

"I need a piece of information, Major Sinclair, and if I really let my imagination run wild, it might prove to be something else entirely. This is in complete confidence," said Mitchell.

"Of course," agreed the major.

"In my capacity as a detective, I've been hired to track down a wayward husband and persuade him to return home." They both smiled knowingly.

"And you want me to tell you where he is?" the major suggested.

"He's needed urgently to sign some very important documents. He usually returns home from these trips after a week but this time he has been gone almost eleven days." The major smiled broadly.

"Perhaps he's found a new more enthralling paramour this time?"

"That is certainly a possibility. The problem is nobody seems to know where he goes in the city and who he sees." Mitchell shrugged.

"And what makes you think I can help?"

"He's only moved into the Peebles area in the last few months although the connection through his wife goes back for centuries. He's a shipping magnate and I hoped that you would keep an eye on the moneyed folk who drift about here. Watch who attach themselves to them from a security point of view I mean."

"Sheddon, James Sheddon, is that him?" asked the major. Mitchell smiled with relief.

"Yes."

"I don't know him or have even seen him as far as I'm aware but he also has business interests in armaments. His name has been flagged up on my list but nothing wrong there as far as is known. But I can tell you this and it is from my intelligence on him, he's no philanderer for apart from this one lady whom he has evidently been true to - his wife won't like that - for twenty odd years, there's nothing of note about him."

"I know, major, that this unknown lady has been recently widowed and I wonder if he has decided to burn his boats and not return home at all. If so, I'll go back to

Crosteegan and hibernate for the rest of the winter after I collect my fee."

"The lady is Mrs Charles McPartlan."

"I thought she was an aristocrat?"

"She is, he wasn't and as an earl's daughter, she's entitled to be Lady Cordelia McPartlan. Seems she's a modern woman and might even be at her club along the street as we speak."

"I hope so for that would allow Maddy Pearson to infiltrate her kitchen and ask a few questions. But if Mr Sheddon is still there, well." But Mitchell had every faith in Maddy. The major scribbled on a page in a small notebook and tore it off.

"The lady's address. Her late husband appeared to have very ambivalent loyalties to the Crown so we kept an eye on him and his wife." Mitchell thanked the major and they both stood up. "And if the errant husband did happen to head for home at the appointed hour?" Major Sinclair asked. Sinclair forgot nothing.

"Then there's a dead body one of my footmen found in Eddleston and then lost that might just be our man from Peebles," said Mitchell darkly.

"Very intriguing." Major Sinclair suddenly stopped by the door and gave Mitchell a piercing look before speaking. "How is Miss Pearson?" he asked out of the blue. Mitchell had forgotten that that pair had met briefly on another case. "Maddy?"

"Yes Madeleine, how is she? Is her ankle better?" Mitchell hid his surprise at this aristocrat's interest in Lord Askaig's skivvy.

"She's alive and well and minding everyone's business, thank God, but, of course, I'm speaking as her employer in The Mitchell Detective Agency not as Lord Askaig's butler." Both men laughed.

"Please give my very best regards to Madeleine," said Major Sinclair as Mitchell once more faced the chill air.

Maddy looked first along the well-designed row of town houses, back down at the little fragile piece of paper and wished Major Sinclair's writing was more legible. That little lunch-break when she had met up with Mitchell after her hospital appointment had been very satisfying. Tea, toast and poached eggs. Mr Mitchell had said he would eat later perhaps but right then Maddy was to eat and he would tell her what he had discovered from his private sources which were to remain private. Thus Maddy never knew that the handsome major had remembered her. She was now to visit Mrs McPartlan who might have already reverted to being Lady Cordelia and try and inveigle her way into the kitchen as a skivvy from a grand house in Peeblesshire who was wanting to climb the promotion ladder. Lord Askaig's household was so pleasant to work in that nobody left. But Maddy most certainly did not want to remain a skivvy all of her days. She had decided to blend fact and fiction when it came to explaining why she had chosen Mrs McPartlan's house. Right then she had not thought about it but would be well-prepared by the time the cook quizzed her mercilessly as cooks did.

Maddy slipped quietly down the steep steps to the basement and round to the back door that led directly to the kitchen. A deep breath and with Mrs Brady's testimonial lodged safely in her bag, she knocked confidently on the door. It was opened almost immediately by a young harassed-looking girl and Maddy recognised a skivvy when she saw one.

"Would it be possible for me to have a word with Cook, please?"

"Are you selling something?" The skivvy was shouldered none too gently out of the way by a pert, confidant kitchen-maid whose hair, face and even apron shone like a beacon. Mrs Brady would have been very suspicious of that one, thought Maddy running a professional eye over her. "We don't buy from vagrants."

"Neither do my employers Lord and Lady Askaig of Crosteegan Castle. The cook, miss, would you please ask her if I could have a minute of her very valuable time." The aristocratic connection came in handy, it seemed, even in this very modern lady's household.

"About what?"

"A position but in His Lordship's great household it's his cook who would be asking these questions when someone from another castle arrives at her kitchen door."

"As it should be," came an irritated voice and Maddy was in. Cook gave Maddy the once-over, noted the roughened hands, short clean nails and highly polished but well-worn boots. "So it's Lord and Lady Askaig? Crosteegan Castle you're from, is it?" Maddy nodded and explained her reason for wanting to leave the castle.

"I have a testimonial from our cook, Mrs Brady, Mrs Jenny Brady." said Maddy handing over the treasured paper. The cook laughed loud and long.

"So she's still at the castle is Jenny Fleming - as was. Jenny went to Lord and Lady Askaig's when I went to the Earl and Countess of Grantcoe, your mistress's parents. That was a long time ago. How is she? Did Jenny suggest here?"

"Yes, ma'am," Maddy lied and felt more than a little guilty. Maybe Mrs Brady would explain later.

"McNiece, Mrs McNiece," said the cook.

"Well, Mrs McNiece, Mrs Brady had heard about Mrs McPartlan's bereavement and as some staff don't like a change of master - if that should ever happen - Mrs Brady thought you might want to keep me in mind should such a thing ever happen." Maddy felt she was beginning to ramble and quickly took refuge in respectful silence.

"It might happen soon in an unofficial way and in that case, more than the kitchen maid will be departing, I can tell you, girl. Lady Cordelia is not one for convention so we might just find ourselves with a new master in jig time without the preliminary ceremony." Maddy made a great show of carefully folding and putting her testimonial from Mrs Brady back into her small bag.

"Maybe I should be going, Mrs McNiece, for I'm not certain that your new - well, maybe - master could compare favourably with Lord Askaig."

"Oh don't you bother about Mr James Sheddon for he's well away for another wee while. Left on Tuesday. Late train so he wasn't exactly anxious, was he? A potentially extremely lucrative meeting, he told Lady Cordelia, was all planned so he had to be there."

"That's a relief, I must say. It would be different if I was here by appointment but just coming on the off-chance, well," Maddy faltered.

"Let's have a cup of tea and a biscuit or two, dear."

"I'd love that, Mrs McNiece but I'm going back to Eddleston by the late afternoon train but I'll be sure to tell Mrs Brady how you're doing. I must say that your kitchen is much smaller than ours but you have it beautifully organised." Maddy knew all the right things to say to a cook.

"Thank you. I came here with the mistress when she married Mr Charles all these years ago. Lovely man, he was. Tell Jenny I'll write." Maddy left with a pot of marmalade and some shortbread for Mrs Brady and some tablet for herself. She liked Mrs McNiece and now felt quite guilty for deceiving her. But Mrs Brady would make it all right when the whole business was over.

Maddy hurried along Princes Street to Waverley Station where it had been arranged for her to meet Mitchell. Her ankle still hurt and she wondered if it would ever be right again. She thought of what she had to tell her employer, Mr Mitchell, of The Mitchell Detective Agency. Maddy was still bursting with pride at having been employed by him as one of his detectives. So Mr Sheddon had in fact left Mrs McPartlan's establishment on the Tuesday. Then where had he gone after that? She felt inside the paper bag and took out the tablet wrapped in its special paper. Mr Mitchell had been working hard as well and had probably not stopped to eat. He could have the tablet. She crossed Princes Street, the busiest street she had ever seen and hurried on past a row of eating houses and shops, into Waverly Station then down to the platform quickly slipping the tablet back inside the paper bag. On second thoughts, Maddy decided, the sweetness of the tablet might just be a step too far for Crosteegan's butler's digestive system after having afternoon tea with a lady friend.

Mitchell sauntered along the platform twenty minutes later and Maddy quickly joined him.

"The train's been delayed, Mr Mitchell. Don't know why. Another thirty minutes that official over there said." Mitchell nodded.

"Then I think we might as well have a report-back right now. Is the waiting-room crowded?"

"Yes because of the cold air."

"Well, over by that pillar will do. How did it go? Did you discover anything?" he asked eagerly.

"Did you?" asked Maddy.

"Nothing more than what I told you my contacts could come up with," said Mitchell.

"I got inside the house," said Maddy, "that is to say the kitchen and it seems the cook is an old friend of Mrs Brady's"

"Really? So you got as far as talking to the cook herself?"

"Yes, which was just as well for the kitchen-maid was all for slamming the door in my face." Mitchell frowned his disapproval at that.

"But the cook intervened, I take it?" he suggested.

59

"She did. A very pleasant woman who seems to think that Mr Sheddon will be their new master shortly, legally or otherwise. Seems Lady Cordelia's a free spirit - free with everything." Maddy blushed and a short silence followed as she once more became skivvy to Mitchell's butler and Lord Askaig's butler suffered no loose talk. Mitchell was first to break the silence

"And is James Sheddon really first in line?"

"If you mean the future sort of bidey-in, yes. And I also learned that he left for home on Tuesday, late train, as planned. Had a lucrative meeting arranged." Planned! Mitchell's brain was turning over at speed. Maddy saw the change in him. "What are you thinking, Mr Mitchell?" she asked.

"I'm thinking, Maddy, of the possibility that our missing husband and missing body might just be the same person." Maddy gasped.

"That's impossible! Why would he be anywhere near Eddleston? Angleford House is on the outskirts of Peebles."

"He wouldn't be the first man to fall asleep on a train, wake up confused and get off at the wrong stop," said Mitchell.

"But who would kill him? Nobody could have known he would get off there, sir."

"Then again, Maddy, perhaps he had arranged to meet someone in Eddleston. Perhaps that meeting was to take place there," Mitchell suggested.

"The someone who murdered him?" Maddy suggested.

"That's right but we need to find that body."

"I wonder if they have, the search party I mean. I wonder if Mrs McNiece will be lucky after all in her new master. She was so pleased to hear about Mrs Brady again."

"I don't think 'lucky' is the word you should be using in connection with someone's death, Maddy." Maddy duly apologised.

"I wish the train would come," she said at last as Mitchell had retreated into thoughtful silence once more.

"Come on," he said at last, "there might not be any seats available in the waiting-room but at least it will be out of the wind and into some small degree of heat."

As they walked along, Mitchell noted the voiced annoyance of the 1st class ticket holders in their own select waiting-room and smiled grimly on noticing they had opened their waiting-room door to let out some of the heat from the roaring fire. Voices, male and female, seemed to become more irritated as Mitchell drew level with the open door and for the second time that day, the past rose up to greet him. He was satisfied for he could now put two things together, voice and face, but to whom did they belong? He stopped a porter he knew well from Lord Askaig's frequent visits to the capital.

"The gentleman wearing the dark grey travelling cloak. I've only met him once or twice at the castle," lied Mitchell, "and I don't want to offend him if he asks me to arrange transport for him at Eddleston. Don't want to address him wrongly."

"Oh, don't bother about the chance of doing that, Mr Mitchell, for it won't happen. That's Lord Kilmanton. He bought the Low Souldress estate a few months ago as you know and he'll definitely have his own carriage waiting for him." Kilmanton was on the guest list for the Old New Year party and must have arrived at Crosteegan as Mitchell had been dealing with the old Dowager. That was why they had never met. The train finally pulled into the station exactly thirty minutes late.

"We were held up, Mr Mitchell," shouted the train driver, a cousin of Archie Newton's, as the train slowly eased to a halt, "because of your Roly Whitehead in a way. They found the body he said he saw - on the other side of the tracks."

Chapter 5

Twilight was fading fast. Only the harsh brightness of the snow still lying thick on the surrounding countryside gave some light to the station at Eddleston and the village street. The platform failed to clear as normal especially on a cold winter's late afternoon. Little groups gathered, split and reformed as the news of the finding of the body spread like wildfire among both passengers and those there to greet them. There were none of the men from the estate around and Mitchell concluded that they were back at Crosteegan. He wondered exactly what had been discovered along with the body. It must not have been more than an hour or two beforehand if the train had been held up whilst the body was recovered and brought across the tracks and then along to the village. Perhaps by now it had been taken to Peebles where there were facilities for keeping corpses.

"Mr Mitchell!" A shout but a subdued one at that and Mitchell broke out of his reverie.

"It's Roly, Mr Mitchell," said Maddy as she drew level with him," he's over there. He would like a word with you, it seems."

"I see him, Maddy. You walk on up to the castle with him if he's not wanted right now by Constable Paterson. It's too cold here and I might be some time as I want to speak to the constable. Things to do. You arrange a table conference with Mrs Brady after the family have had dinner and the other servants dismissed. Just you, me and Cook. Actually I have a feeling we might need Jude Donaldson to work on the case so get hold of him." Mitchell turned Roly aside as he hurried along the village street to meet him.

"I told you, Mr Mitchell, didn't I that he was dead right enough. The doctor's been and says he's probably been dead for two or three days. But they will know more accurately than that when the official medical man at Peebles has a good look at him."

"Come on, Roly," said Maddy taking him firmly by the arm, "Mr Mitchell says we've to get on with our own work and he'll have a word with Constable Paterson. As you're still getting fed at Crosteegan, you can help in the kitchen this evening. Keep well out of sight of the family." But Roly was too wound up to listen.

"Found him on the other side of the railway, Mr Mitchell. How did he get there? The animals had a good feed off him they say but there are no night prowlers strong enough to drag him there from where I last saw him, Mr Mitchell. Did the murderer do it? But why?"

"Work, Roly, Lord Askaig's good nature will only go so far and you're not permanent anymore." Maddy prodded Roly along until they were once more heading along the village street and then onto the road that ran from Edinburgh to Peebles. Mitchell watched till they had crossed the little bridge and then were out of sight. Roly's point had been a good one. Why had the body been moved? Why would a random killer find the need to do that? And more important still, was it in fact James Sheddon whose body, Mitchell presumed, now lay in the police outhouse? The temperature was so low no harm would be done keeping it in Eddleston till the following day. The temporary police surgeon, Mitchell knew, would be in no hurry to come out on a night like that to perform his duty. Mitchell knocked firmly on the door of the police station and waited.

"I've been expecting you, Mr Mitchell. Come right in." The station was part of the constable's house and Mitchell could feel the warmth filtering through from his living quarters. "Come right into the office out of the chill. You've heard the news then?" Mitchell nodded and the policeman shook his head. "It's a bad day when a peaceful place like this is the talk of the county because of a vile murder."

"Then it was definitely murder, Constable Paterson?"

"No doubt about it. The foxes and their friends brought in the Old New Year in style but there was enough left of the smashed skull to tell it was a human hand yielding a blunt instrument, as the doctor called it, that caused the death. Human wrong-doing, it was the result of that."

"I'm told the body was found some distance from where Roly saw it."

"About one hundred yards. We found the exact spot where the man fell before being dragged along to and over the railway line. Roly came up trumps this time. Easy to find the spot again as it was directly opposite the path leading to Portmore Loch."

"Do you have any idea who the victim is?" asked Mitchell. "None. Could give you his height and weight roughly and colour of hair. There it is, all written down. Nothing on him to identify him. A broken index finger on his right hand but that was a recent injury and whether it was due to the attack or not, the medical man in Peebles will be able to say for certain. Our doctor thought that there were signs that a bandage had been round it for a while but you know him, very reluctant to commit himself. All he has to confirm, he says, is that the victim is officially dead. I think we have a huge problem on our hands, Mr Mitchell."

"Possibly not."

"What?"

"I have a feeling that I might just know someone who can identify the victim."

"Do you think you know the deceased?"

"No, not personally, but I think I can contact people who might be able to if I have your permission. No names right now as it's all very confidential and sensitive but, suffice it to say, the person or persons will be accompanied by Mr Cairns of Peebles."

"The Writer? The solicitor?" asked the policeman.

"Yes. Now do I have your permission, Constable Paterson, to send him a note asking him to bring along those people and enclosing a copy of your description?"

"Certainly and the sooner the better. I must say that the help I've had from Lord Askaig and his servants today has been outstanding. I think it's best that we put Roly Whitehead's actions yesterday down to just an honest mistake. In his hysteria, shall we say, he made a genuine error."

"We are in your debt at Crosteegan, constable. I feel that in helping identify the unfortunate deceased, it might go some way to repaying that. I noticed that Geordie and his cab are still by the station."

"Hoping for a fare off the late train to Edinburgh, no doubt."

"Quite so. As that won't be for some considerable time, he should manage to deliver this message to Peebles and return in plenty of time to meet the train." Mitchell produced his small leather notebook and wrote his letter to Cairns. "May I trouble you for an envelope, Constable Paterson, and some wax?" The message was duly sent.

"Would you care to view the victim, Mr Mitchell, or will you stay and go in with Mr Cairns' people?"

"If the dead man is who I think he is, then there would be no point as I have not made his acquaintance. No doubt if he is this person then Mr Cairns will be able to provide you with all the information you will need. He will be able to do the preliminary identification himself and save the people he brings with him unnecessary anguish if it proves to be a false alarm. I'll be on my way to Crosteegan. Will you keep me informed at the castle, please?"

"Certainly, Mr Mitchell. It's just dawned on me that this is the first time the Crosteegan team has won the curling match." Mitchell laughed and put it down to Roly paying much more attention than usual to tactics knowing that if he was found out in his initial lies he would need all the goodwill he could muster from Lord Askaig. Too bad he had not mustered quite enough despite being tactically astute that afternoon.

Mitchell's eyes took in everything as the footmen served Lord Askaig's dinner guests. There were thirty seated at the dinner-table and he had inspected every placing, every piece of crystal, every flower on that table beforehand. Perfection. Mrs Brady's contribution was a triumph as always and Mitchell relaxed a little as the conversation round the table flowed easily. His mind wandered briefly as the dinner-party ran smoothly along well-oiled lines. His thoughts drifted back to that half-remembered face and slightly high-pitched voice as they had come together, jolted into his consciousness by an irritated complaint about the lateness of the train that afternoon. Lack of punctuality was disgraceful and, it seemed, would not have been allowed to happen on the railways in India despite the almost unimaginable drawbacks. Mitchell himself was more than satisfied with the trains and understood that really bad weather was bound to affect the running times. But that particular overdue train whose delay was due to police activity just outside Eddleston had been more than welcome as it had allowed Mitchell to put voice to face and identify the owner of both. He had been wrong for he had indeed met Lord Kilmanton before, long ago, in India when a short-lived insurgency, preceding the Mutiny, had meant a detachment of The Black Watch had been hemmed in for four days outside Lucknow with some civilians. Now who would have thought Mitchell would meet one of them again while both were living around a small village like Eddleston. All there had endured one entire evening of listening to the whining voice of Mr Christopher Riley of the East India Company, deep in his cups, as he swore repeatedly that if he lived through the present danger he would never rest until he had killed the man who had ruined his life in every way imaginable. Riley had obviously prospered spectacularly after that incident and managed to get himself a peerage to boot. Mitchell also wondered if that threat made so long ago had ever been carried out.

Mrs Brady placed the plate of warm scones on the table beside the butter and blackcurrant jam and then sat down before pouring tea for Maddy, Mitchell and herself.

"It was Lord Askaig's name that got me through the door of Lady Cordelia's house and your testimonial that got me a seat at the kitchen table, Mrs Brady," said Maddy.

"I taught Dotty McGregor how to make rumbledethumps when we were very young and she taught me how to make Ecchlefechan Butter Tart," said Mrs Brady smiling at the memory. "Mr Mitchell, this football match against The Black Watch, I take it you'll be wanting me to provide the catering."

"That I will, Mrs Brady, and a nice little earner it will be too. I'll tell you the actual date a week in advance as Major Sinclair has given me two to choose from. That let's me find out when the boys will be free. Now, Maddy, did you speak to Jude?"

"Not yet, Mr Mitchell, as he's working at Home Farm but should be back any time. I've left word that he's to come over here as soon as he can to speak to you." Maddy looked dead on her feet and Mitchell would have told her to get some rest but he knew her terrier instincts would have been outraged. "These scones are delicious, Mrs Brady," said Maddy. "I'll bet even the White Goose Teashop at Waverley Station doesn't serve ones as good as these, do they Mr Mitchell?" asked Maddy smoothing jam artistically over the butter on each half of her scone.

"Over-rated, ladies." Clipped tones.

"Too many windows, too, I think," said Maddy enjoying her imagined image of the butler's stern face for she assiduously avoided actually looking at him.

"Your scones are excellent as always, Mrs Brady." Mitchell had been found out and he was furious.

"Didn't Mrs McNiece give you a cup of tea and a scone or a pancake seeing as how it was a testimonial from me you were carrying, Maddy?"

"She did offer, Mrs Brady, but I was in a desperate hurry as I had to meet Mr Mitchell at Waverley. I didn't want to keep him waiting in that bitter cold. I know he doesn't like waiting-rooms so I waited for him outside in case he thought I was late." Mitchell's feelings turned to the guilt Maddy had intended and went into overdrive. He changed the subject immediately.

"Mrs Brady, I wonder if you would cast your mind back a good few years." The cook's interest was immediately aroused.

"Are we talking, Mr Mitchell, about the doings of The Mitchell Detective Agency?" she asked.

"We might be, Mrs Brady. Until we have a positive identification of the body, it's just interest, nothing more." Mrs Brady and Maddy nodded in unison. Maddy wondered where it was all going and what had sparked a new line of enquiry in her agency boss's mind. Mitchell weighed up how best to put it without damning someone's reputation unnecessarily. Sheddon's character intrigued him. What had two high-born women seen in him that had instilled a lifelong love and yet revolted the servants in Lady Cordelia's household. Perhaps it was simply loyalty to a much-loved master. But who in fact were Mr and Mrs James Sheddon? Mitchell was constantly on the alert for Constable Paterson's knock on the door. He felt ashamed, but only momentarily, at wishing the body was that of James Sheddon. He wondered if Mrs Sheddon would over-ride Cairns' sense of decency and insist it had been the local constabulary that had found her husband and therefore no fee was required by Mitchell.

"I'll do my best, Mr Mitchell. I've a very good memory so on you go." The cook and Maddy sat back and waited.

"Angleford House."

"Yes, the entire estate was owned by Sir Michael Lindsay when I was a girl. Had been in that family for generations as I told you. Still is, of course although it's been many a day since they've lived in the house."

"Do they still own the estate, Mrs Brady?" asked Mitchell.

"Lock, stock and barrel. Moneyed, that's what they are, always have been. Louisa Lindsay married into money and then inherited all her father's wealth as she was the only offspring of her parent's marriage. She's Mrs

Sheddon now and they've recently come back to live at Angleford."

"Was Sheddon a landowner hereabouts, too?" asked Mitchell. The cook shook her head.

"Not that I know of. He had relatives in the district but came originally from Glasgow, yes, definitely Glasgow, although I think he'd lived for a time in Edinburgh. There was a lot of talk, of course, at the time. She was young and beautiful - had any number of suitors to choose from."

"But she chose him. Gift of the gab, had he, Mrs Brady?" Maddy suggested.

"Must have had, Maddy, for he was nothing to look at." Mitchell coughed disapprovingly and the women took the hint.

"But she was never one to fall for a pretty face," said the cook knowingly.

"Really?" Maddy's thoughts had returned briefly to what she had seen at the White Goose and slight defiance crept in again. "Why do you say that, Mrs Brady?" she asked. "More tea, maybe Mr Mitchell? Shall I fill the pot again, Mrs Brady?" Maddy rose and fetched the kettle to make fresh tea while Mrs Brady spread butter and jam on another few scones.

"Fetch some pancakes as well, Maddy. It all boiled down in the end to a straight battle for her hand in marriage between two of them, James Sheddon and Christopher Riley."

"And Sheddon won," said Mitchell thoughtfully. "Why?"

"Was it love, Mrs Brady?" asked Maddy returning with the large teapot.

"Her father had the casting vote the story went and Louisa didn't seem to mind which one got it. Maybe she thought life amongst the Glasgow shipbuilding community would be more exciting than somebody whose money came from trade. Just as well in the end for Riley was declared bankrupt some months later."

"I wonder if her father had an inkling of what was in the wind," Maddy suggested biting into a currant pancake.

"Sure to," answered Mitchell, absently putting too much sugar into the large cup of tea that the cook kept specially for His Lordship's butler. "Was he ever seen in the neighbourhood again?" he asked.

"Not that I know of. Louisa Lindsay married and I presume Riley's thoughts turned to financial matters." Mitchell desperately wanted to know if Mrs Brady had ever seen Lord Kilmanton but he certainly did not want to connect him at that moment with the murder victim if James Sheddon was in fact the deceased. Mrs Brady and Maddy were nobody's fools and he knew that they were already thinking that Sheddon was Mitchell's bet for the victim. If it did turn out to be him, then Mitchell had already decided to pay Mr Airley, owner of *The Peebles Clarion*, a visit. He would have made it his business to be up to date with the background of a new resident of note in the county and a Peer of the Realm such as Lord Kilmanton certainly came into that category. Mitchell had the intuitive feeling that Lord Kilmanton was indeed that former employee of the East India Company, Christopher Riley, who had sworn vengeance on an unnamed man who had ruined him in every possible way. But he needed proof that the two names belonged to the same man. Had a love lost and bankruptcy been the twin evils heaped upon him by the mysterious person? A loud rap sounded at the door and Maddy showed Constable Paterson into the kitchen. Beckoned by Mrs Brady to join them and suitably furnished with tea and scones, the Crosteegan trio waited in silence for the news the policeman had come to deliver.

"Bad day for Eddleston, Mr Mitchell, Mrs Brady, Maddy." Rank was something a policeman understood.

"Then the victim is a local resident, constable?" Mitchell had taken the lead as was his right in that great household. The policeman nodded and swallowed loudly.

"I expect you know without being told now, Mr Mitchell. Your guess, I should say deduction, was absolutely accurate."

"Are we, Maddy and I, allowed to know the identity, Constable Paterson?" asked Mrs Brady.

"No reason why you shouldn't, ladies, as it will no doubt be all over the county by morning as the relatives who identified the deceased, the murdered man, will have been recognised if not by their appearance for they were all shrouded - wrong word there, sorry - in voluminous clothes but by their carriage. The horses will have given the game away." Mrs Brady slipped a hand on the edge of the plate of scones. Constable Paterson knew what was required to release it. "Mr James Sheddon of Angleford House." The plate was passed silently towards him.

"Now who would want to kill the poor man, Mr Mitchell, and however did you reason that one out? Remember, Maddy, all spoken round this table is in confidence, it goes no further." Maddy frowned at the implication and the cook made up for the unintended insult by opening a tin of toasted macaroons.

"Mr Cairns employed The Mitchell Detective Agency," explained Mitchell, " to seek out Mr Sheddon at his Edinburgh club in order to let him know that business matters of great urgency required his presence at home. Mr Sheddon had been in the habit of visiting various friends in the city and occasionally stayed overnight with them instead of returning to his club if the weather was inclement." They all nodded and pretended to believe him. "The one main fact that Maddy and I discovered which confirmed that Mr Sheddon had indeed left Edinburgh on Tuesday but had never arrived home, made me suspect that the body might be his."

"But surely," said Mrs Brady, "he would only have left the train once it had reached Peebles?"

"That is something I can't explain at the moment," said Mitchell shaking his head. "Perhaps he woke up confused and thought he was at Peebles. Right now, I don't know." But the constable had more information.

"I think perhaps I can clear that up, Mr Mitchell. Do you remember the broken finger? Well it seems that it happened a fortnight ago whilst Mr Sheddon was out riding. He was thrown from his horse when the animal refused to take a hedge. In the fall, Mr Sheddon broke his finger and lost consciousness for several minutes. It could be that he was still suffering from the effects of that fall and, as you say Mr Mitchell, he probably woke confused and simply got off at the wrong station and completely lost his bearings. It seems to me that he was most unfortunate to stumble across a vagrant in the woods and was assaulted and robbed by him. He would be in no physical condition to defend himself." All three of his listeners nodded.

"That would seem to be a reasonable conclusion, Constable Paterson," said Mitchell trying to decide when he could manage to slip away from the castle and go to Peebles the next day. He was simply not convinced and yet the whole episode was obviously pure chance. But then, out of thousands of soldiers and millions of civilians in India, chance had brought Mitchell, Lord Kilmanton and death threats together and Mitchell thought it would be churlish to ignore it.

Chapter 6

Roly was pleased. Mr Sheddon had been the victim of a murderous attack by a tramp. Wrong place, wrong time and the culprit almost certainly, as declared by the constabulary of the county, now long gone from Peeblesshire. Roly could relax and Crosteegan could settle down again. Lord Askaig had offered Roly his job back as he had been suitably impressed by the young man's concern in returning to help the victim and Roly had jumped at the offer.

Mitchell alighted from the very short train journey to Peebles and made his way smartly to the offices of *The Peebles Clarion*. Their files would be more up-to-date than those of the library. He also wanted to insert an advertisement telling of the upcoming fixture between his football team and The Black Watch, date, place and kick-off time to be announced within the week.

"Good morning, Mr Mitchell, another game on the horizon, I take it?" said Henry Airley, the proprietor and editor, as Mitchell quietly closed the door of his littered office. Every surface, every inch of what could have been termed free space was covered in foolscap notebooks or essential reference volumes and back copies of the newspaper.

"This one will be the biggest crowd-puller to date, I'm happy to say, Mr Airley," said Mitchell perching on the edge of a stool.

"And will keep the wolf from the door for a week or two, Mr Mitchell," said the editor perched on a similar seat.

"More than a week, much more than a week." Even donating part of it to charity as agreed with Major Sinclair would still leave Mitchell with enough money to be in a position to plan ahead with confidence. "So an advertisement it is but just a preliminary one to start with stating only the intended fixture but that all details will be published within a week or so. A bit of a teaser, so to speak, Mr Airley."

"Sounds very intriguing but it seems to me that it must be a famous team to generate a lot of money and not many of them will agree to play what is a very good side but not compared with those in the big cities." The editor wanted to be enlightened.

"It's the size of the support that counts and this one will bring with it the largest one there is."

"You've got me there. Mr Mitchell. The name of the team?"

"The Black Watch." Henry Airley whistled. Mitchell smiled broadly.

"And the regiment is stationed at Edinburgh Castle. They'll bring the entire regiment here with them for support. I take it you'll be playing here in Peebles, Mr Mitchell?"

"I'm counting on that, Mr Airley. Venue here still to be negotiated. Now, I've written it out. Put a border round it, if you please." Mitchell passed the paper over to Airley.

"I certainly will, That's always the first item my readers go to. It's attention-grabbing." The editor looked it over, wrote a few printer's instructions on it and money changed hands.

"I'll be in touch as soon as I have the full details," said Mitchell rising.

"That intimation you placed a few weeks ago changing the team's name to FSV caused quite a stir. Since you gave no hint as to why it was changed to FSV, we had a lot of people writing in with suggestions for it." Mitchell laughed.

"That was a great idea of yours running a 'Guess what FSV stands for' competition especially when you don't know the answer," said Mitchell.

"But you're going to tell me Mr Mitchell in return for information, aren't you?" They both laughed. Newspapermen were very wily creatures Mitchell had always found.

"That I am but only when the competition closing date has arrived. Will you trust me on that one? By the way, what's the prize?" asked Mitchell.

"I'll trust you and the prize is lunch at The Golden Horn for two. My wife's the cook there and she gets a staff discount."

"Now I wouldn't mind winning that one myself." Truth to tell, only Maddy, Major Sinclair of The Black Watch and Mitchell himself new what the initials stood for and the major had agreed to keep it to himself as Mitchell had initially toyed with the idea of a pay-to-enter competition himself.

"So what's the question, Mr Mitchell?" asked Mr Airley and sat back and waited.

"As Lord Askaig's butler, I have to be well up on his visitors' and guests' backgrounds for many reasons which I'm sure you understand." Mitchell had used Henry Airley's vast knowledge before. The editor nodded. He was also aware that the two men had exchanged information before and Henry Airley thought Duncan Mitchell a very wily man. He pretended to believe what Lord Askaig's butler was telling him and Mitchell knew it.

"Guests' needs," added the editor, "wants, likes, dislikes, background are all required by a butler in a great house so that he never puts a foot wrong."

"Precisely. The problem is that at the moment, as quite a few of our surrounding estates have changed hands recently and one or two of the new owners are very private individuals, my team of under-butler and footmen are floundering a little for want of that background information. Let's just say some of them have no long pedigree that I can check out for details. We've had no blunders as yet but being prepared as best we can eliminates that sort of pitfall."

"Quite so, quite so."

"I have a list here with one or two sketchy family backgrounds needing to be filled in. Quite innocuous but Crosteegan runs so smoothly and successfully by being prepared. His Lordship expects it." The list changed hands, the editor scribbled the required information and Mitchell folded the paper into his pocket-book and prepared to leave.

"That last bit about Lady Windford's cousin should explain a lot," said the editor trying hard to suppress a smile. Mitchell laughed.

"A great deal indeed, Mr Airley. I expect Mrs Brady and friends have already been speculating. You should be working in Fleet Street."

"Like you, Mr Mitchell, I leave nothing to chance and suspect everything and everyone. Perhaps I should be working for The Mitchell Detective Agency." Mitchell nodded. He thought that that might be an excellent idea, on a casual basis, of course.

Mitchell walked slowly along to the offices of R&D Cairns, Writers to the Signet, his mind keenly focused on the affairs of Christopher Riley, Lord Kilmanton. So the eternal triangle had come together once more as Fate dealt the cards. Had the winner become the loser and vice versa this time? Impossible, or was it? No, thought Mitchell, it was perfectly possible. Would Lord Kilmanton make a move to win the fair lady's hand now that his rival was well and truly off the scene? Had he even had a hand in ensuring the wife was now the widow? But, thought Mitchell a little disappointed, there was no way that Peer of the Realm could have been in two places at the same time. Mitchell asked himself as he strode along the broad and most attractive High Street why he did not just let it go. A passing vagrant, it must surely have been that and he firmly believed that Sheddon had left the train at the wrong stop because his head injury had made him disoriented. But yet that memory of an evening long ago in India when army personnel and civilians were forced in to each other's company would not leave him. A drunken, bitter man repeatedly voiced his intention to kill another man who had seemingly ruined his life. Mitchell now knew for certain that that man in India so long ago had been Lord Kilmanton and the man who had thwarted him at least in love was now dead. Had Sheddon also caused Kilmanton's bankruptcy? Then again, there was no way he could have killed Sheddon that evening. But Mitchell's mind just had to explore even the most remote possibility. At least the visit he was about to make to Mr Cairns would be beneficial to him from a financial point of view. The Agency would have earned some money and Mitchell would have gained an insight into another aspect of Lord Kilmanton's life. If he thought it would benefit his client in anyway, Roger Cairns would be only too happy to give Mitchell information. The Lindsay estate was vast and successful and he would want very much to keep the legal side of the business.

Mitchell was shown in immediately to the senior partner's office having passed through the respectful silence of several clerks working steadily at their desks. Only the clatter of a typewriter being worked in another room told that R&D Cairns, old established business though it was, was willing to embrace modernity if it were efficient. Mitchell thanked the chief clerk as he left the two men to conduct their business in private.

"I have your cheque here, Mr Mitchell, according to your instructions of last evening. Mrs Sheddon appreciates your help in this matter and was most insistent that you should be paid immediately." Mitchell pocketed the cheque with due thanks.

"It grieves me, Mr Cairns, that there was such a tragic outcome to the case," he said.

"The family are naturally devastated as am I, Mr Mitchell."

"I quite understand for I know you've been the family's solicitor for a long time," said Mitchell.

"For over thirty years and our father before us."

"I thought Mr Sheddon was not from this county?"

"You're right, of course, Mr Mitchell. I was meaning Mrs Sheddon's family, the Lindsays. Mrs Sheddon has always been our client even after she left the district when she married."

"That was long before I came here," said Mitchell.

"You were in The Black Watch, I hear - a sergeant, I believe?"

"I was."

"I'm from an army family myself although my younger brother and I followed in my father's legal footsteps. My two older brothers were both in the Coldstream Guards." Mitchell smiled.

"As befits Borderers, Mr Cairns."

"Yes. I'm told you were in India at the time of the Mutiny?" Mitchell nodded. "It must have been awful."

"The heat and the kilt were definitely that but the rest was all part of army life. They say that Lord Kilmanton was in

India, too, at one point," said Mitchell now the conversation was beginning to turn his way.

"Another of my clients of long standing. His Lordship awarded this firm his business when there was some hope of him marrying in this area. Yes, he was in India, so he tells me," agreed the solicitor.

"But not with the army? No forced marches in intolerable heat?" Mitchell suggested innocently.

"With the East India Company. He went out to make - I should say remake - his fortune."

"Remake?" Mitchell hoped his surprise sounded genuine.

"The deals he made out there the first time meant that he was set up financially for life. Turned over all his legal business to us as he intended to remain for the foreseeable future in the county. That was about twenty years ago or so."

"So what went so wrong that he lost it all? I'm assuming that happened as you said 'remake' his fortune. I'm not asking for confidential information, you understand, Mr Cairns. I know that you would never betray a client's trust just as my lips are sealed regarding any unguarded moment's talk I hear as Lord Askaig's butler."

"There was nothing confidential about certain aspects, Mr Mitchell. The whole county knew that there were two rivals for the hand in marriage of Miss Lindsay and that, quite obviously, James Sheddon won."

"I take it, by implication, the rejected suitor was Lord Kilmanton?"

"Correct. He was simply Christopher Riley in those days. But it was not just the romantic aspect that soured relations between all concerned." Cairns was obviously unsure now of what constituted what had been in the public domain at that time and what was confidential family business. "We've always been the Lindsay family's solicitors as I told you but not Mr Sheddon's. I believe his legal affairs are in the hands of a Glasgow firm. Mrs Sheddon owns the entire estate but she is wealthy only in property. She is very attached to the land."

"But Mr Sheddon has money to spare?" Mitchell suggested.

"I believe he has probably left Mrs Sheddon very wealthy in the monetary aspect too." Solicitors apparently spoke freely to each other. "His solicitors will be formally in touch soon as they have a branch in Edinburgh and a finger on the business and social pulse. It would all seem to be very straightforward."

"As you say, Mr Cairns, these affairs become public knowledge very quickly. But how did Lord Kilmanton manage to lose his money?" asked Mitchell very anxious to acquire this particular piece of information, "and how soon after the romance ended in disappointment?"

"A loan, Mr Mitchell. It appears he loaned someone money, a considerable amount, in fact almost all he had and the recipient of his largesse failed to repay it."

"But surely the loan must have been covered legally in case of such an eventuality?" Mitchell was quite shocked.

"It should have been," said Cairns with great disapproval, "and knowing Christopher Riley, it almost certainly was but..." Cairns stopped talking and just shrugged his shoulders.

"And he didn't sue?" asked Mitchell.

"No trace of any action being raised. Curiosity and immense disbelief made me pursue it, Mr Mitchell." Mitchell sighed,

"And so to the East India Company and fortune. A very substantial one today, it seems."

"Beyond your dreams and mine, I think." Cairns looked round his premises which had probably changed not at all in fifty years except for the sound of the typewriter.

"Do you think the agreement between the two parties could have been a simple note, quite informal, between friends?" asked Mitchell.

"That is definitely the only conclusion to be drawn. My brother David and I looked at it from every angle and that's the conclusion we came to for Mr Riley was saying nothing which in itself was very unusual when a business deal had gone wrong. Definitely not a way to be recommended when conducting business."

"So there is no way of knowing who was the cause of his financial ruin?"

"None." Cairns laughed suddenly. "Maybe these days Mr Riley, Lord Kilmanton, feels grateful to whoever it was for it was almost certainly the deed that eventually led to his present fabulous fortune." Mitchell thought that perhaps Lord Kilmanton did indeed eventually feel that way but he was aware of one thing the solicitor was not. The one who ruined Kilmanton financially was also the one who had bested him in love and James Sheddon was murdered less than a mile from where Kilmanton had been at the time.

"Perhaps Miss Lindsay had heard rumours. I'm told that the lady was equally enamoured of both suitors."

"It certainly seemed that way at the time. Another rumour was that her father steered her in the direction of the financially sound James Sheddon," said the solicitor.

"Perhaps Sheddon had made the talk of Riley's precarious financial position known to Sir Michael?" Cairns was quick to put two and two together.

"Now hold on a second, Mr Mitchell. Don't you be tying Lord Kilmanton into this murder as a possible act of revenge. If Kilmanton harboured a grudge at all over his treatment as a suitor then it would be against the lady's father not Sheddon. Sir Michael was obviously the one who manipulated it all and Sheddon the innocent bystander." Mitchell nodded his head slowly.

"So within months," said Mitchell, "Kilmanton lost both love and money. No wife, no loan being repaid." Mitchell could see the sense in Cairns' argument. Sir Michael would have been the object of Kilmanton's hatred, not Sheddon. But there was still something about it all that Mitchell's instincts could not let go. He decided to puzzle it all out over a good plate of soup and some bread and cheese at The Golden Horn Hotel so he left the solicitor's office deep in thought. He had been paid for his and Maddy's work yet he still somehow felt he was short-changing the dead man's widow. Mitchell had never undertaken a simple missing person case before because the clientele he had were of such a station in life that it was almost impossible for them to go missing without dropping completely out of sight of the society they lived in and into much inferior living conditions. Their very upbringing made that, however desirable the idea of opting out of life's problems might seem, completely anathema to them. They were too used to being at the top of the heap that complete anonymity somehow had to include staying there.

Mitchell's thoughts were interrupted by Maddy's clear voice.

"Mr Mitchell!" A quiet call but an effective one. "A word, please." Mitchell drew her under the columns of the Chambers Institution. He waited there to hear the reason she was in Peebles and not in the scullery at Crosteegan Castle.

"What is it?" He hoped she had some fresh information, about exactly what he did not know. Just something, however small, that would send his mind off on a train of thought that he knew was close-by but completely obscured by facts that did not matter.

"Mrs Brady says to tell you that Captain Andrews would like, if you would be so kind as to make it for him, a…"

"Chicken curry," Mitchell finished for her. "Yes, I'll be back in time to do that."

"Mrs Brady also says would you write down the spices needed and I'm to buy them in Copland's. Here's a list of the ones she already has."

"I will," and Mitchell duly added the missing ones. "Anything else, Maddy?"

"Jude has returned to the castle and I spoke to him as you're in Peebles and he's wanted back at Home Farm. They're clearing out the spot for a new vegetable garden.

Lady Askaig wants to expand it considerably, he said. He told me, sir, that Lord Kilmanton was dropped off about half a mile north of Portmore Loch that night of the Old New Year celebrations. He told his coachman the roads were too icy and as they had skidded a few times, he was nervous and decided to walk the rest of the way. The carriage was to be taken to Crosteegan and he would be driven home after the ball. Roly arrived back long before him, Jude said, for everybody noted the state he was in." Mitchell's delight at this new information raised his spirits high.

"So Lord Kilmanton could have been at the Portmore Loch turn-off at the time of the murder. Maddy, did I tell you I'm very glad to see you?" Maddy smiled wryly.

"No, sir, never in my whole time at Crosteegan." But she knew Mitchell was no longer listening to her. She also knew that she could change that within seconds. "Jude also said that he was helping to fix the lanterns around the forecourt when Lord Kilmanton appeared behind him still wearing his heavy cloak. He's certain Lord Kilmanton arrived much later than a careful walk along the road would have taken. I've just seen Lord Kilmanton enter The Golden Horn, sir." She definitely had Mitchell's attention now.

"Maddy, you should know that I have been paid by Mrs Sheddon so you will receive your pay in a few days and we'll forget the fact that you foolishly offered to forego it. Never offer to do that in business deals, Maddy. Now its time I had a bite to eat. Off you go and shop for Mrs Brady."

"Do you think he did it, Mr Mitchell? She asked, still standing by his side.

"He?" asked Mitchell.

"Lord Kilmanton. He's always wanted her."

"She turned him down or at least her father did."

"And she didn't protest?" said Maddy sceptically.

"That's right."

"And why? According to Mrs Brady, Miss Louisa Lindsay as was ruled the roost at Angleford House. What she wanted, she always got."

"So she must have wanted and got the glittering life," said Mitchell.

"Nonsense. Money can buy you that and the Lindsays were well-heeled, they say." Mitchell smiled at his young assistant detective. Maddy was very astute. He now wondered how Louisa Lindsay knew about that loan and how it would not be repaid for in Mitchell's mind now, that lady knew Christopher Riley who was courting her would be bankrupt within months. Had she and Sheddon, who was known for investing heavily in large engineering projects, somehow swindled Riley? Had Riley given Sheddon that loan? Was the loan made in return for leaving the field open for Riley, as Kilmanton was then, and Sheddon had reneged with Louisa's full approval?

"In answer to your question, Maddy, yes, I'm almost certain he did and I'm about to get him to convict himself."

Chapter 7

Mitchell cast his eye round the many rooms that led off the reception area of the celebrated Golden Horn Hotel in Peebles' High Street. The quiet buzz belied the fact that the dining-room was full and the bar well-occupied too.

"Is Lord Kilmanton here?" asked Mitchell. The manager, well-used to Crosteegan's butler dropping in whenever he was in Peebles for some of the hotel's famous roasts, nodded and pointed to the lounge-bar door.

"Far corner. His Lordship's alone but he's hired the small parlour for lunch for himself and several guests."

Mitchell entered the room, the gentle hum of conversation in marked contrast to the more boisterous The Wild Duck. The clientele here was more of the gentlefolk class. He watched as Kilmanton slowly enjoyed his malt whisky before approaching him.

"Excuse me, Lord Kilmanton, but if I may, perhaps I might ask you a question or two on behalf of my employer, Lord Askaig. I am his butler." A title six hundred years old was definitely one up on one a mere nine months in existence.

"Certainly, em." Kilmanton struggled to remember Mitchell's name before abandoning the attempt.

"Mitchell, Lord Kilmanton. My under-butler was on duty when you came to the ball at Crosteegan on the Old New Year's Eve. An empty silver card case was left behind after Lord and Lady Askaig's Old New Year party. We were wondering if it belonged to you, sir." Kilmanton shook his head decisively as Mitchell knew he would.

"Mine is gold. Did it have initials on it?"

"No it did not, I'm afraid, which is why we're having great difficulty reuniting it with its owner. We will eventually manage it but when I saw you enter this hotel, the idea that it might belong to you sprang to mind." Kilmanton looked incredulous.

"What? Are you saying a silver card case with no initials on it immediately reminded you of me?"

"I'm sorry if you are offended, Lord Kilmanton, but it was actually a little more than that. It is a very beautiful card case of superior workmanship," lied Mitchell who was, in truth, not above a lie or two himself when circumstances called for it, "and the embossed design of peacocks and acanthus leaves are obviously of Indian origin. It is a fine piece and quite obviously made in India, probably by jewellers to one of the maharajahs. I know you were in India at one point and simply linked the two. I thought it would be a good starting place for finding its owner. Obviously I was wrong."

"My career with the East India Company was spent almost exclusively in Hong Kong and Macao." Mitchell smiled.

"Almost but not quite, Lord Kilmanton. Am I correct?" Kilmanton looked closely at Mitchell and then laughed.

"You are. I was told that the Crosteegan butler knew everything about everybody," he said without malice.

"They exaggerate," said Mitchell modestly, he hoped.

"Well, you are correct. I was in India very briefly a long time ago on company business and have almost, I'm happy to say, erased that experience from my mind."

"The trouble near Lucknow? Now there I can't fault your lordship for wishing to forget that." Kilmanton looked long and hard at Mitchell but failed to solve the puzzle.

"Were you also there at that time?" Mitchell nodded.

"An unforgettable experience," he said.

"Civilian or army?" asked Kilmanton.

"Army."

"Must have been The Black Watch then. I only met those soldiers once and very few of them at that. It's all rather hazy. I expect I had too much to drink. Dutch courage, I'm afraid. And you were there in that tiny compound?" Kilmanton wondered.

"In the local official's's house for eight long nights. Sergeant Mitchell."

"Fresh from the Crimea."

"That's right, Lord Kilmanton."

"So you connected my somewhat tenuous link to the subcontinent with a little silver case of Indian design?"

"That I did for you were a Mr Christopher Riley in those days and not quite in the gold trinkets league then, sir."

"Come on, Mitchell, let's talk out the demons in private. I have guests coming for luncheon, Mrs Sheddon, her aunt and my secretary who is fetching them. But they'll be a good fifteen minutes yet. We can talk over old times over a dram in the small parlour unless Lord Askaig requires your presence."

"Not for quite some time, Lord Kilmanton. Captain Andrews is residing at Crosteegan for a few weeks with his wife, our Lady Jane, and he's asked that I make him his favourite curry in the true manner of a soldier who learned the secret in India itself." The two men moved through to the privacy of the small parlour and a bottle of Laphroig was produced and poured. Mitchell, being a true Ileach, never refused a drop of the sublime whisky from his native island. Kilmanton was first to speak.

"I do indeed recall that terrifying experience, Mitchell. As a soldier, no doubt you were different in your reaction to the murderous situation we were in."

"The difference, Lord Kilmanton, is in discipline and in the knowledge that that is the only real asset you have in these situations. It simply lets you concentrate on the real issue."

"I don't think I quite made the grade on that occasion for I vaguely remember drinking too much," said Kilmanton.

"And talking roughly the same." Kilmanton looked up quickly from his glass and looked closely at Mitchell's inscrutable face.

"What's this all about?" he asked sharply. Fear had etched itself on his own features and Mitchell wondered if this situation was not new to him. Perhaps in his younger days he had been indiscreet in business matters and been the subject of blackmail. But the consequences of this matter would be much more dangerous to Kilmanton's self-preservation than throwing money at a blackmailer.

"You're a businessman - magnate - Lord Kilmanton and I'm an ex-soldier who has probably seen more of the worst of human nature than most. In other words, straight talking is second nature to both of us."

"So what did I say all those years ago that's made you finally approach me?"

"You said that one day you would kill the man who had ruined your life both in love and finance." Mitchell knew that Kilmanton had been too drunk that night to remember his exact words and he finished the rest of his whisky before looking once more at Mitchell.

"And how many men have vowed that when drunk and riddled with fear. Any hope of a future at all would be comforting. It was all just a drunken ramble on my part. Now I think Lord Askaig's butler can go back to his master and tell him that the silver case, if it even exists, is not mine and then you will be free to take your place in the castle kitchen and cook that curry." Mitchell smiled and did not move. He had heard all that kind of bluff before.

"Not yet, Lord Kilmanton, not just yet. There are a few minutes left before your guests join you. The man you intended killing that long, terrifying night in India was indeed murdered when you were no more than yards away and probably, of course, battering the life out of him." Mitchell waited while the accusation sank in and saw shock and fear follow each other fleetingly across the other man's face. The silence seemed to last forever before Kilmanton was finally composed enough to answer.

"We're talking about James Sheddon, I presume," said Kilmanton all of his self-control being used to keep his voice steady.

"We are," said Mitchell quietly.

"And you have proof to back up this accusation? The police have been informed of what I can only call your fanciful ideas culled from a hazy diatribe over ten years ago?"

"No to both questions, Lord Kilmanton. You were turned down by Miss Lindsay in favour of Sheddon and he also featured in a loan that was never repaid to you."

"All supposition. Miss Lindsay was free to make her own choice and my financial affairs in no way and at no time included James Sheddon. You can search all legal avenues you can access, Mitchell, and you will find no proof that we ever had any financial dealings. Likewise, if, as you say, I was in the vicinity of the place when Mr Sheddon was murdered, then it was purely by accident and I knew nothing about it. The roads were extremely icy and I had my carriage driver let me alight some distance from the Crosteegan lodge and I walked the rest of the way. Nothing at all happened during that journey and I arrived safely and had a very enjoyable time. As far as I know, and all of the County of Peeblesshire too, Mr Sheddon was there in that wood near Eddleston as a result of some disorientation so premeditation is out. I'm also told by the family that Sheddon was bludgeoned to death but I think Lord Askaig's own servants will tell you that I only needed my boots spruced up a bit from walking in the slush made by traffic on the road. Not a trace of blood on my clothing." That thought had also bothered Mitchell but he held his ground as Kilmanton tried to usher him out of the door.

"You never walked up that drive to Crosteegan, Lord Kilmanton. You came from across the parkland, a completely different direction. And that mistake, Lord Kilmanton, will be your undoing." Mitchell could not figure it out right then. Kilmanton must have passed by the lodge and on towards Peebles. But why? Mitchell moved towards the door as Kilmanton spoke once more.

"I killed James Sheddon, Mitchell? You will never prove it but feel free to try," he taunted. "Now get out!" Jude had mentioned that this man had come up behind him. It might have meant nothing at all as he could simply have been avoiding some carriage ruts for Jude had obviously been concentrating on the lanterns. That had been a shot in the dark by Mitchell but it had changed Kilmanton's demeanour from being relatively relaxed to now throwing him out. The Mitchell Detective Agency owner was well-pleased with his time spent in Peebles.

"Good day, Mrs Sheddon." Mitchell stood aside in his best butler manner as the widow entered the small parlour. "My most sincere condolences, madam." Mrs Sheddon paused and smiled wanly as she thanked him.

"Lord Kilmanton has suggested a little air and a light luncheon to help." Mitchell moved on as the tears welled up in the still beautiful face and were blinked back. He nodded to whom he supposed was Kilmanton's secretary and Mrs Sheddon's aunt as they closed the door behind them. Mitchell was more determined than ever to find the proof that would show Kilmanton up for the murderer he really was.

Mitchell walked back along the High Street and heading for Northgate. He had the feeling that inside The Wild Duck lay the answer to the whole mystery. He hoped that the one man with the information he badly needed was still there. If Mitchell was right and he admitted to himself that he was going on pure instinct, Kilmanton would face a murder charge and right beside him would be his dining companion, Louisa Sheddon.

Chapter 8

Mitchell walked under the archway guarding the courtyard of The Wild Duck and made his way into the lounge-bar. It was packed as usual at this time of day, noisy, smoky and welcoming. He felt the old excitement rise in his stomach. So much depended on what Dodie Spiers had to say. Mitchell had accused Lord Kilmanton of murder and the consequences for him would be catastrophic if he were wrong. His gut feeling now told him that Kilmanton and Mrs Sheddon had planned it together but he had no real proof whatsoever. No doubt money was at the root of it all. Was Sheddon's money not enough not for her compared with the great fortune Kilmanton had amassed out East? Had a life among the shipbuilding fraternity palled compared to the exotic one she assumed Kilmanton had lived and would continue to live with her beside him? Had a former lover's presence proved too corrupting for both of them and her ambition and his bitterness together made an explosive mixture and it was the betrayer, Sheddon, who was blown away? Also this way, Louisa got to keep his fortune and the use of another. Somewhere in Mitchell's mind that posed another question and a possible answer. Dodie had been in earlier and Mitchell fervently hoped he would still be there and when he spotted the Brangle lodge-keeper, his relief was almost palpable, his dread almost as great for there was really only one answer Dodie would give him that would save Mitchell and condemn that vile pair. There was no going back now.

"Hello Dodie, how are the babies?" Dodie Spiers broke off from speaking to his friends and turned and joined Mitchell at the bar.

"Fine, thanks, Mr Mitchell, as is Lizzie."

"Could I have a quick word with you, Dodie, in private?" asked Mitchell at the same time ordering another of the same for the lodge-keeper.

"Surely, sir." Mitchell led Spiers to a quiet corner and they both sat down on an old wall-bench that ran round three walls of the room. "How can I help you?" Spiers accepted his drink from the landlord, thanked Mitchell and then waited with a countryman's patience for Mitchell to begin.

"The night the babies were born you say you spent most of it pacing up and down outside the lodge."

"Aye, that I did."

"You also said all traffic ceased after the carriages obviously going to the ball at Crosteegan passed."

"The ladies were all dressed up in their finery, best cloaks, and in high spirits. I could see their carriage lanterns turn right in the distance as they went through the lodge gates. The usual coaches that passed by regularly tailed off and then ceased."

"The ladies and their escorts certainly enjoyed themselves, I can tell you that, Dodie," said Mitchell laughing at one or two memories of that evening. "Dodie, I want you to cast your mind back to that night once more. Think hard, Dodie, for it's very important. Did you see anyone actually walking along the road?" Dodie thought for a moment or two.

"I'm told some of His Lordship's guests preferred walking to the castle from the other side of Eddleston but not coming up from Peebles, they didn't. I can swear to that. There were some of the Eddleston lads going to have a drink here in Peebles who waved as they passed and Old Eddie and his wife came down from Brangle as usual after he had been cutting wood for the estate. His wife helps out with the laundry. That would be well before the carriages began to pass bound for Crosteegan, though. But after that? Well, I can't be sure of a couple of folk some little time after the last of the guests from this side of Eddleston had passed. It was a dark night only really lit by the snow lying hard on the ground for there was very little moonlight to see by. I had just gone to the lodge side door for a hot drink and some buttered bread to eat outside when I spotted them." Mitchell felt his breathing almost cease. "A man and a woman. They were all huddled up, just shadows really. They were already about fifty yards along the road going hurriedly towards Peebles. A most unwise way to move with the road being in the state it was." Mitchell took a deep breath before speaking.

"Did you recognise them, Dodie?" But Dodie shook his head and took a long sup of his ale. "Both of them?" Dodie shook his head. "Too dark and too far away. They were all wrapped up in heavy, dark clothes as it was a very bitter night." Mitchell's hopes were shattered.

"But I did wonder why Louisa Lindsay was walking. Never known her to walk any distance and we were children together." The tension in Mitchell rose as he asked the vital question.

"Mrs Sheddon?" Louisa was not a common name.

"Aye, Louisa Lindsay. My father was a gardener on that estate just like me on Brangle. Lodge-keeper and gardener, that's my job. I grew up with her. Would know that walk of hers a mile off, even on a dark night."

"And the man with her?" But Spiers shook his head.

"That's the problem. Sorry, Mr Mitchell, I've no idea." Mitchell knew that was almost inevitable as Kilmanton's appearances twenty years before had been sporadic and equally scarce now. "I heard about Mr Sheddon. A bad day right enough, Mr Mitchell, but I must say I thought him a sly weasel when he was courting Louisa. I wouldn't trust him as far as I could throw him. You'd never get me on one of his ships, I can tell you." Mitchell laughed.

"Can't see one sailing up the Eddleston Water looking for business so you're quite safe, Dodie. Take care and my regards to Lizzie."

Mitchell had it all straight in his mind now and he felt that the make or break moment had come when he saw Constable Paterson and the local police inspector walking towards him.

"A word if I may, gentlemen?"

"Certainly, Mr Mitchell. You know Inspector Gracie?"

"Of course. Good to see you, Lawrence," said Mitchell smiling.

"Many thanks for your help in all this Duncan," said the inspector, a loyal FSV supporter and occasional player. "Is it about a future fixture?" asked the policeman hopefully. "Any chance of a game?" Inspector Gracie was a sporadic wonder in goal and as the regular one had just injured his knee at work, there was every chance of it.

"Definitely but first, I wonder if you would step into this lane and listen to what I have to say regarding the murder of James Sheddon." Mitchell spoke with deliberate clarity and without haste as he outlined what he felt sure had happened and watched as the expressions on the faces before him changed from mere interest to incredulity.

"What would you like us to do, Duncan, for I know that actual evidence is not very strong and you have something definite in mind in the way of action?"

"It's a case of prompting thieves, or in this case murderers, to fall out. I simply want to confront them with my version of what took place and why and see how they react. With you there, it will at least help to keep them in the room. Lord Kilmanton is obviously an excellent businessman with a steady nerve in these matters but I know from first-hand experience that he falls apart when under physical pressure and being hanged for murder is certainly in that category." The inspector knew he had nothing to lose as the case had more or less been put down to the work of a vagrant because of the random nature of Sheddon's being there at that time and they were having no success in tracing the murderer. It was also playing merry hell with his clear-up statistics and that meant a lot of snash from his superiors. If Duncan Mitchell was wrong and a terrific fuss ensued as it certainly would, thought Gracie having fallen foul of the upper-classes before, he was well-versed in talking his way out of it and his football manager would be pulled through unscathed by Lord Askaig.

"Go on," he said, knowing Lord and Lady Askaig's butler's presence at Crosteegan Castle was worth more to them than hysterics from some Johnny-come-lately Peer.

"Lord Kilmanton, Mrs Sheddon, his secretary,"

"Alasdair Clerk," said Constable Pearson helpfully.

"And her aunt,"

"Mrs Houston. She lives with them and Mr Clerk was her husband's secretary for a long time until Mr Houston died last July." The constable was well up on the social scene of his district and had been disappointed at having been summoned by Inspector Gracie to be told that they were standing down some of the officers on the case.

"Thank you, Constable Paterson," said Mitchell. "They are all in a private room right now in The Golden Horn Hotel and I'd be grateful if we could have a word with them in your presence as Inspector of Police, Lawrence." The inspector nodded his agreement and the three men entered The Golden Horn.

The total silence as Inspector Gracie spoke told Mitchell he was up against very determined and dangerous people. The only person in shock was the aunt, Mrs Houston, and her husband's ex-secretary was doing his best to keep her quiet nervousness from building to a crescendo.

"Lord Kilmanton, Mrs Sheddon, there have been allegations made against both of you," said the inspector, "of a most serious nature."

"Concerning what, Inspector Gracie?" asked the widow in the softest tones.

"And by Lord Askaig's butler I presume from his presence here," suggested Lord Kilmanton, his voice dripping scorn as he spoke.

"Concerning what?" repeated Mrs Sheddon still seated as were her lunch companions at the now-cleared dining-table. The three interlopers were ranged just inside the door.

"I think that will become quite clear as Mr Mitchell's theory progresses for, at the moment, it is just that, a theory.   By listening to him air what are serious accusations in this more informal setting than."

"Than what?" interrupted the secretary.

"Than at the police station nearby," barked the inspector in the most acidic tones and it was clearly his view that he could be completely frank with a fellow-worker whereas he had to tread cautiously with the wealthy. "Mr Mitchell, let's waste no more time here.   Please let's have your accusations or allegations and the reasons for making them so that the two people concerned may, if they wish, repudiate them."   Gracie stood against the door with his arms folded and Mitchell did as he was bidden.

"James Sheddon died last Tuesday evening but the events that led to that murder, for there's no denying that that was what it was, all began some twenty years before right here in Peeblesshire. Two men vied for Louisa Lindsay's hand in marriage. Those men were you, Lord Kilmanton, then

Christopher Riley, and the late James Sheddon. Miss Lindsay, as you were then Mrs Sheddon, was the only child of Sir Michael Lindsay whose family had owned the Angleford estate for generations."

"And still do," put in Mrs Sheddon tartly.

"Indeed it does. The catalyst in all of this sorry tale was a loan, a private one. Although I have no material proof of this, I am convinced the loan was made by you, Lord Kilmanton, to Sheddon in return for a promise to leave the field clear for you as regards courting the lady and a subsequent marriage. It is widely known hereabouts that the loan was never repaid, you went bankrupt and James Sheddon, supposedly moderately wealthy at the time, flourished in the shipbuilding boom in Glasgow, no doubt helped along by his new financial boost. In short, James Sheddon not only reneged on the deal, he went on to marry Miss Lindsay shortly afterwards." Lord Kilmanton sat shaking his head and smiling slightly.

"I've already stated, Mitchell, that that is errant nonsense and that you'll find absolutely nothing in the way of paperwork to back up your ridiculous supposition."

"And I wonder why that is?" said Mitchell.

"Because I didn't loan Sheddon any money. I went bankrupt simply because a business decision I made was the wrong one. The only time in my life that I have done so," Kilmanton added smugly. "The consequences were catastrophic to me but that was many months after James Sheddon and Miss Lindsay were engaged to be married. The lady preferred him to me. Simple as that." But this time it was Mitchell who was shaking his head.

"No, Lord Kilmanton, there's nothing simple about any of this. There is a devious mind or minds behind it all," he said confidently but in fact his own mind was verging on turmoil. Something was wrong, very wrong about that loan and he could not work it out. Kilmanton was bluffing, Mitchell was certain of that, but he could also recognise the truth when he heard it and there was more than a grain of it in what Kilmanton had said. But in which part? Mitchell had no alternative but to continue. "You'll forgive me, Lord Kilmanton, if I reveal an episode in both our lives to the ears of the rest of those in this room." Kilmanton's face was like thunder as he guessed what Mitchell was referring to.

"Do I have a choice?" he asked sarcastically.

"I'm afraid not. Our journey into the past now takes us to that colourful and intriguing sub-continent, India, at the time of the Mutiny, when Lord Kilmanton was still an employee of the East India Company, and I was a soldier stationed near Lucknow. While under siege and the odds stacked against anyone surviving, His Lordship took refuge in the bottle whilst the more experienced men and women there put their faith in their firepower and good discipline. During those long, fraught nights until we were relieved, that same East India Company employee continually vowed to kill the man who had ruined his life in love and finance. Regardless of Lord Kilmanton's protestations, I firmly believe that that man was James Sheddon and that it was not only Lord Kilmanton who murdered him but that his accomplice in achieving that act of bitter revenge was the woman the two men had fought over originally, Mrs Sheddon." Kilmanton immediately sprang at Mitchell but the financier was no match for an ex-sergeant and was very roughly shoved back into his seat.

"How dare you make such an accusation against this lady," Kilmanton yelled. Mitchell looked away from him and gazed at Louisa Sheddon, her face now as white as the linen cloth on the dinner-table.

"Are you really suggesting that I killed my dear husband, Mr Mitchell? How could I and why should I?" said the widow quietly.

"I'm suggesting exactly that, Mrs Sheddon. Whilst the actual murder was taking place, I have no doubt you were there and it's perfectly possible you wielded perhaps a stone to stun Mr Sheddon. After that, it would be easy enough to finish the deed. But I suspect you were more of a lure and that Lord Kilmanton performed the more physical aspects." The old aunt passed out and Alasdair Clerk struggled to haul her out of the room.

"No, Mr Clerk, leave her be," said the inspector as the lady began coming round again. He helped the secretary place her gently back on her chair. "She might be a witness in Mrs Sheddon's favour and we can't be seen to show favour to one party nor to seem to be prejudiced against anyone either." The elderly lady was now slumped in her chair and holding a glass of water rather shakily in her hand. Kilmanton was furious.

"This is outrageous, Mitchell. I'll ruin you, you can rely on that," he vowed.

"Not by smashing my head in you won't as you have obviously done to another man you swore vengeance on. Bear in mind, sir, that no-one emerges from a war-zone quite the same mentally as he went in and I've been in more than my fair share of them." Two could play at that game, thought Mitchell.

"Are you threatening me?" hissed Kilmanton rising once again.

"If you attempt revenge Christopher Riley-style," replied Mitchell, "it's a promise not a threat. Now get back into that chair and stay there." Inspector Gracie was quick to try to restore better relations.

"This is only just people talking the situation through," he said attempting to pour oil on troubled waters. "I'm sure that Mr Mitchell will be only too pleased to receive explanations for any allegations he has made. Better clarifying these in private for, as we all know, mud sticks. Continue please, Mr Mitchell." Gracie was giving Mitchell much more leeway than he should and he knew it. But he had heard the rumours of a big football game coming up and he desperately wanted Mitchell to pick him for the team. Mitchell knew that too.

"I used the word 'lure' for that's exactly what I believe happened on Tuesday evening. You, Mrs Sheddon, lured your husband to his death."

"But how could I possibly have done that? My husband was missing. Overdue. I hired you to track him down. I was at home in my room distraught the whole of that day," said Mrs Sheddon perplexed.

"It was a clear case of James still suffering from his head injury and a vagrant coming across him in the woods," said Mrs Houston in strident tones. "We were all upset at his disappearance and no-one more so that Louisa." Mitchell ignored her.

"James Sheddon got off that train in Eddleston not by chance but by appointment. He was expecting to meet his wife and go to Crosteegan Castle." Mrs Sheddon shook her head as Mitchell spoke.

"My husband refused to socialise in the county," she said defiantly. Mitchell smiled wryly.

"He would when multi-millionaires and the aristocracy were involved," said Mitchell sourly. "Did you tell him he could change into the appropriate clothing at the lodge? That they would have been left there earlier for him?"

"This is absurd," said the widow. "I didn't know where he was in Edinburgh or even if he was there at all. How could I contact him?"

"I found out within an hour of being in Edinburgh. I'm sure Lord Kilmanton, having renewed his friendship with you, would have volunteered the services of his numerous contacts in the city from his days in the East. There's quite a colony of them in the capital. Success was virtually guaranteed. Hiring me was just a public display of fake concern." But Kilmanton was quick to dispel that one.

"Mrs Sheddon and I have only met socially on a few occasions since I have been back here. She was, no doubt, too sensitive to presume on what was a recent resumption of our friendship. Mitchell, I strongly resent your attempts to bully the lady."

"I'll note that point, Lord Kilmanton. Now, if you will let me continue." Mitchell was surprised that the fierce fury that Kilmanton had displayed earlier had now dissipated a little. Was the physical reality of his situation now coming into play? "Mrs Sheddon, I think." But he got no further.

"Yes, you think," said the widow mimicking Mitchell and smiling at Lord Kilmanton whose mind seemed to be slightly sluggish just then for he did not respond. Some of his spirit had gone. Mitchell ignored the interruption.

"You didn't expect to see him until that Tuesday evening at Eddleston. It had all already been arranged between you and your husband secretly before he even left; Eddleston, the late train, the change of clothes, the business meeting and James Sheddon walked right into the scene of his own death. What excuse did you give him for the secrecy? Pulling off a last-minute deal at someone else's expense? It had all been planned with you for that was the word he used to Lady Cordelia, planned. But Lord Kilmanton also knew that this so-called disappearance was a sham, a story put about by you. The two of you had decided to kill him, Lord Kilmanton because of the bitterness eating away at him and you to obtain a free hand with his money. It could be used to buy back parts of the estate sold by your father." Mitchell looked at Kilmanton and the man's demeanour increased the feeling that he was wrong somewhere in his reasoning and that frightened him a little.

"My niece was at Angleford all day," said the aunt firmly.

"No she wasn't, madam, for both Lord Kilmanton and your niece were seen heading south towards Peebles after the time the murder had been committed. There is no dubiety about that." The agonised silence that followed Mitchell's statement stretched for some minutes with Mitchell desperately trying to figure out where he had gone wrong, where his blending of fact and fiction was beginning to unravel. Suddenly Kilmanton spoke and broke the tension in the room.

"I was indeed in the woods, Mitchell, but Sheddon was already dead when I got there."

"Liar!" shouted Louisa Sheddon. "You told me to do all that. You told me to get James there, told me what to say about discussing a potential business deal with Lord Askaig that night. He threatened me, Inspector Gracie, threatened to kill me. You've heard how good he is at that. He said I was to tell James when he got off the train that the carriage was waiting near Portmore Loch as it was the only safe place to turn. The shortcut through the dry ground of the woods would be quicker. He had always hated James. He killed him. I saw him do it. It was awful," wept Louisa Sheddon. "My poor darling and I couldn't save him for it was all so sudden." Kilmanton looked as pale as death. He finally found his voice.

"What are you saying? My word of honour, Inspector Gracie, I was walking towards the castle lodge when Louisa came out of the woods. She was distraught and told me that Sheddon had dragged her into the woods and tried to kill her but a tramp had come to her rescue and Sheddon was dead. She said Sheddon had suddenly accused her of having an affair with me and he would kill her before he would let me have her. She was weeping and almost fainting. She said she would explain it all to me later, how she got there, why she was there, how the horse had bolted and begged me to accompany her back to the outskirts of the Angleford estate. I said I would fetch my carriage but she said she wanted no-one to know that she had even been there. I didn't kill him. I've never killed anyone. I only walked her back to Peebles where she insisted I leave her near Angleford House."

"And you went to Crosteegan across the parkland?" asked Mitchell. Kilmanton nodded.

"It was a quicker way to the castle. It was very dark. Nobody noticed or so I thought."

"Yes." Louisa Sheddon suddenly spoke again and her voice sounded gentle and composed once more. All eyes were now on the widow as she spoke. "Lord Kilmanton didn't kill him. I didn't kill him either. He did!" she suddenly screamed. Alasdair Clerk made a bolt for the door but Constable Paterson felled him with one blow of his large hand. The old lady threw the remains of her glass of water over her husband's former secretary as the constable hauled him to his feet and thrust him back into his chair. "He'll deny it, of course. He'll lie about everything," shouted Mrs Sheddon, "for there's not a single bit of truthfulness in his body." Louisa had remained seated, Kilmanton now leaning, appalled, head in his hands on the table as the implications of it all sank in. Mitchell was equally shocked.

"Shut up!" It was good advice from her aunt and Louisa took it. Inspector Gracie was next to recover.

"I think perhaps Lord Kilmanton should clarify a few points before we all move on to the police station. Constable Paterson, I think we'll wait here until you fetch a few of your colleagues along. Also see to it that Mrs Sheddon's solicitor, Mr Cairns, is informed." The constable departed in haste with a threatening glance back at Clerk. "Mr Clerk, you begin for it's you whom Mrs Sheddon has accused, then Lord Kilmanton next and Mrs Sheddon, take your aunt's advice until Mr Cairns appears." The secretary's hope of escape had gone. He ignored Louisa Sheddon and looked straight at Mitchell.

"You were right when you said it had all begun a long time ago. We were lovers, Louisa and I, from the first day I was in her uncle's employ. It was before she was married. Sheddon and Riley meant nothing to her but their money did. Sir Michael was in financial difficulties and Sheddon persuaded him to ask Riley for a loan of a large sum of money. Riley, Lord Kilmanton now, gave it and received a signed note in return."

"Lord Kilmanton, is this true?" asked Mitchell. Kilmanton looked up.

"Yes."

"And what happened to that note?"

"Sheddon burned it in front of me before I could stop him. I now had no proof I had ever given money to Sir Michael. I assumed Sir Michael was also in on it so there would be no use speaking to him about it. I've often wondered how Sheddon got hold of it." He stopped talking as the truth dawned on him and he shook his head before moving on down the table away from Louisa Sheddon. Clerk confirmed his worst thoughts.

"Louisa had it. She was supposed to have seen to its being put safely in Cairns' hands. Sir Michael knew nothing of it being burned. Sheddon told him that he had paid it back for him as he and Louisa intended marrying so the old man was delighted." Louisa Sheddon's soft laughter cut into the silence that followed. She knew that nothing would stop Clerk from telling all.

"Were they then working together, Sheddon and Miss Lindsay?" asked Mitchell.

"Yes, in a way. It meant she could have Riley's money and access to Sheddon's by marrying him. Of course, she was also in line to inherit the Angleford estate. She had it all planned out. They were both fools where she was concerned, Sheddon and Riley, or should I say Lord Kilmanton?"

"And you were party to it all?" Mitchell suggested.

"I knew about it, yes."

"And you continued to be lovers?"

"Why do you think Sheddon sought solace in Lady Cordelia's company? He got none at home. But he was a worm, a crawling apology for a man. He deserved all he got. You can't respect someone who would ruin another man in his presence. There are standards of decency, you know." Mitchell and Gracie looked at each other in undisguised amazement. "Lord Kilmanton was telling the truth when he said Sheddon burned that note in front of him. He did it that way just to see the horror in his rival's expression as the fact dawned on him that he had given his entire fortune away and ruin was staring him in the face. There was now no proof of that loan ever having been made. Sheddon laughed whenever he recounted that story."

"So, Mr Clerk," said Mitchell, "what part did Lord Kilmanton play in James Sheddon's death?"

"None. Seems he got off to walk as Louisa and I were about to leave the woods. I had left the dog-cart further up the path to Portmore Loch, well-hidden from anyone who ventured along that way that night, and planned to take Louisa back most of the way to Angleford and then she could sneak back into the house. Sheddon had staggered away after the first few blows from me and that's when the Crosteegan footman saw him." Mitchell inwardly groaned. "So he really was asking for help when the footman thought he was simply making weird moaning sounds?" he suggested. Poor Roly. This would make him hysterical again.

"Yes," said Clerk, " but I got hold of him and finished him off." There was no emotion there, no regret and it crossed Mitchell's mind that he was talking to a real monster. Roly had been right. There had been one in those woods that evening.

"And so Mrs Sheddon blundered into Lord Kilmanton that evening?" suggested Inspector Gracie. Clerk nodded.

"And I must say the fool is as gullible today as he was twenty years ago," said the widow spitefully. Kilmanton's eyes told of a sorrow that would last a lifetime.

"And you ran after Roly Whitehead to finish him off."
Mitchell was filled with anger. But Clerk shook his head
at Mitchell.

"No. I was still hiding among the trees. Louisa had
picked up a stone as the young man stood watch over the
body. She has no patience, couldn't let it go at that."
Louisa Sheddon felt she should explain her failure to kill
that evening.

"He's very fleet of foot is that young man, Inspector
Gracie, or he too would have gone the way of all flesh."
She was obviously enjoying herself and Mitchell came to
the conclusion she was either mad or knew she could
secure the services of the best advocate in the land.

"Why did you move the body?" asked Inspector Gracie.

"To assure more time went by before the police found it,"
explained the widow. "Given the weather, we thought it
would erase any clues we had inadvertently left behind.
His clothes and his possessions are a soggy bundle
somewhere at the bottom of the Eddleston Water. We
used a heavy boulder to weigh them down. Portmore Loch
would have been better but it's frozen over. Very simple.
Were you all sweating blood over that?" she asked.
Louisa Sheddon then giggled in delight at the thought and
her stern aunt slapped her hard.

"But why?" asked Mitchell of Clerk. "Was James
Sheddon very frugal with his money since money now
seems to be at the root of all this evil?"

"Never that, Mr Mitchell, but we reckoned that if he were
out of the way, Louisa could marry her besotted old suitor
who had obviously come back, unmarried, to live near her.

Instead of having a wealthy husband, she would have a fantastically wealthy one. Pure economics. We had to act then for Sheddon's lover's husband had died a few weeks before and we thought that Sheddon might leave Louisa and her supply of money, while not ceasing, would be considerably reduced."

"And you planned to continue being the cuckoo in the nest," said Mitchell coldly. Clerk smiled.

"But what a nest, Mr Mitchell, what a nest!" He and Louisa Sheddon looked at each other and laughed convulsively.

Maddy finished peeling the mountain of potatoes for dinner and wondered now that Crosteegan's butler had finished making the curry for Captain Andrews if he had perhaps filled a little ashet with some of it for her for he knew how fond she was of it.

"Come through and have a rock cake, Maddy. By the way, I've had a word about that girl and her sewing. You've to fetch her here next Wednesday," Mrs Brady called to her from the Servants Hall.

"Thank you, Mrs Brady. Alice will be very pleased," said Maddy sitting down at the table next to Jude.

"What do you think of this for a business card for The Mitchell Detective Agency, Maddy?" asked Mitchell as he regarded a sketch he had just drawn on a piece of foolscap paper before passing it to her. Jude Donaldson sat opposite him grinning. Maddy took the sheet of paper as Mitchell explained he would be placing it with the printers in Peebles the following day. Maddy read it aloud.

'The Mitchell Detective Agency
The Wild Duck
Northgate
Peebles

Owner and Chief Detective: Mr Duncan Mitchell
Associate Detectives: Miss Madeleine Pearson
                        Mr Jude Donaldson
Discreet and reliable service assured. No domestic
cases accepted.'

"Very good, very business-like, Mr Mitchell," was all she said but she was fit to be tied with pride and delight as there was also a small ashet full of curry at the far end of the table. "But what about poor Lord Kilmanton having moved to be near his love and that woman turning out to be so wicked," she said sadly. She shook head at the thought of unrequited love. Mitchell looked up from surveying his handiwork once more.

"Lord Kilmanton bought Low Souldress to be near his love right enough," agreed Mitchell, "and his engagement to her, our Lady Victoria, is to be announced next week. Keep that information to yourselves." Mrs Brady was first to break the stunned silence.

"A well-matched couple! They deserve each other! Have another rock cake, Mr Mitchell."

If you have enjoyed reading *The Realms of Death* please leave a review on Amazon. Marie Rowan welcomes any constructive feedback.

Other books by Marie Rowan published by Moira Brown:

Mitchell Memoranda Series

Gorbals Chronicles Series

Dom Broadley Series (Young Adult)

Printed in Poland
by Amazon Fulfillment
Poland Sp. z o.o., Wrocław

55426239R00074